F
Sh61b

Shields, Carol.
    The box garden : a novel / by Carol Shields. — Toronto ; New York : McGraw-Hill Ryerson, c1977.
    213 p. ; 23 cm.   C77-001260-4
    ISBN 0-07-082547-5 : $9.95

    I. Title.

PZ4.S55427 Bo   1977   813'.5'4   77-375961
[PR9199.3.S514]   MARC

Library of Congress   78

The
Box
Garden

The Box Garden

a novel by
Carol Shields

McGRAW-HILL RYERSON LIMITED

Toronto   Montreal   New York   St. Louis
San Francisco   Auckland   Bogota   Düsseldorf
Johannesburg   London   Madrid   Mexico   New Delhi
Panama   Paris   Sao Paulo   Singapore   Sydney   Tokyo

THE BOX GARDEN

Canadian Cataloguing in Publication Data

Shields, Carol, 1935-
 The box garden

ISBN 0-07-082547-5

I. Title

PS8587.H489B69   C813'.5'4   C77-001260-4
PR9199.3.S52B69

1 2 3 4 5 6 7 8 9 0 D 6 5 4 3 2 1 0 9 8 7

Printed and bound in Canada.

For my son John

For my son Tobias

Chapter 1

What was it that Brother Adam wrote me last week? That there are no certainties in life. That we change hourly or even from one minute to the next, our entire cycle of being altered, our whole selves shaken with the violence of change.

Ah, but Brother Adam has never actually laid eyes on me. And could never guess at the single certainty which swamps my life and which can be summed up in the simplest of phrases: I will never be brave. Never. I don't know what it was—something in my childhood probably—but I was robbed of my courage.

Even dealing with the post-adolescent teller in my branch bank is too much for me some days. She punches in my credits, my tiny salary from the *Journal*, the monthly child support money (I receive no alimony), and the occasional small, miniscule really, cheque from some magazine or other which has agreed to publish one of my poems.

And the debits. I see her faint frown; a hundred and fifty for rent. Perhaps she thinks that's too much for a woman in my circumstances. So do I, but I do have a child and can't, for his sake, live in a slum. Though the street is beginning to look like one. Almost every house on the block is subdivided now, cut up into two or three apartments; sometimes even a half-finished basement room with plywood walls and a concrete floor rented out for an extra sixty-five a month.

Oh, yes, and a cheque for thirty dollars written out to Woodwards. A new dress for me. On sale. I have to have something to wear on the train. If I turn up in Toronto in one of my old falling-apart skirts, my sister Judith will shrink away in pity, try to press money into my hands, force me with terrible, strenuous gaiety on a girlish shopping trip insisting she missed my birthday last year. Or the year before that.

Food. I am frugal. Seth at fifteen undoubtedly knows about the other families, those laughing, coke-swilling, boat-tripping families in bright sports clothes who buy large pieces of beef which they grill to pink tenderness on flagged patios, always plenty for everyone. Second helpings, third helpings. We have day-old bread sometimes. Bruised peaches, dented cans on special. Only the two of us, but food still costs. It's a good thing Watson insisted we have only one child.

And what's this? A cheque made out to the Book Nook. I had forgotten that. A hardcover book, bought on impulse, a rare layout. Snapped up in a moment of overwhelming self-pity. *I'm thirty-eight, don't I have the right to a little luxury now and then? They never have anything new at the library—you have to sign up for requests and then wait half the year to get your hands on it and this way it comes all swaddled in plastic, you just can't get into a library book the same way, why is that?* Eight dollars and ninety-five cents. I'll have to be more careful. But I'll have it to read on the train.

It's not only bank tellers. Landladies wither me with snappish requests for references.

"And why did you move from the west side, Mrs. Forrest? You say you're divorced; well, just so you pay regular."

And I do. I am my mother's daughter; cash on the line and cash on time. Her saying. She had hundreds like it, and although it's been twenty years since I left home, her sayings form a perpetual long-playing record on my inner-ear turntable.

The squeaky wheel gets the grease. No need to chew your cabbage twice. A penny saved—this last saying never fully quoted, merely suggested. A penny saved: we knew what that meant.

By luck Watson came from a family with a similar respect for cash; thus he has never once defaulted on the small allowance for Seth. The cheque is mailed from The Whole World Retreat in Weedham, Ontario where he lives now. On the fifteenth of every month; no note, nothing to indicate that we once were husband and wife, just the cheque for one hundred and fifty dollars made out to me, Charleen Forrest.

My name, the name Forrest, is the best thing Watson ever gave me. After being Charleen McNinn for eighteen years it seemed a near miracle to be attached to such a name. Forrest. Woodsy, dark, secret, green with pine needles, exotic, far removed from the grim square blocks of Scarborough, the weedy shrubs and the tough brick bungalows. Forrest. After the divorce friends here in Vancouver suggested that I announce my singlehood by reverting to my old name. Give up Forrest? Never. It's mine now. And Seth's of course. I may not be brave but I recognize luck when I see it, and I will not return to the clan McNinn.

McNinn: the first syllable sour, familial; the second half a diminishing clout, a bundle of negative echoes—minimum, minimal, nincompoop, ninny, nothing, nonentity, nobody. Charleen McNinn. No, no, bury her. Deliver her from family, banktellers, exhusbands, landladies, from bus drivers who tell her to move along, men on the make who want her to lie back and accept (this is what you need, baby), friends who feel sorry for her. Deliver me, deliver me from whatever it was that did this thing to me, robbed me of my courage and brought me here to this point of time, this mark on a nowhere map, this narrow bed.

You made your bed, you can lie in it, my mother always said.

※

"You really ought to get into meditation," the Savages urge me as we wait for the waiter to bring us our food.

"Why?" I ask.

They exchange quick, practiced looks of communion. Doug receives from Greta the miniature nod to proceed.

"For true peace of mind, Char," he says. "For release."

"Look," I say in what I think of as my Tillie the Toiler voice, flip bravery mingled with touchiness, "who says I need peace of mind? Or release. I'm not ready to die yet."

"We're talking about serenity," Greta leans over the hurricane lamp so that her tiny, earnest creases are transformed by shadow into grey, lapped folds; a seared, oddly attractive gargoyle of a face. Her pouched eyes plead with me.

"It's really far more than serenity," she urges softly. "It's an answer, a partial answer anyway, to—you know—fragmentation. Isn't it, Doug? I mean, it gives you a sense of your own personhood."

"What Greta means is that it frees you from trivia," Doug explains. "And who, I ask you, needs trivia? You want to trim it off. Like fat off a chop. Cut it out." He sits back, pleased with himself.

Doug and Greta Savage are in their mid-forties. Where do butterflies go when it rains? Where do hippies go when they get old? They get frowsier, coarser, more earnest or more ridiculous like the Savages; they look fun-

4

mick. It's a positive power. By forcing the brain to concentrate on an absurdity . . ."

Greta's tiny mouth puffs into a circle of protest, but he hurries on.

". . . by forcing the brain to concentrate on an absurdity, you let the mind go free."

"What exactly do you mean by 'free'?" I ask. My question is not frivolous, nor am I stalling for time. Free might apply, for instance, to any of Greta's passions over the years—free love, free bird houses to the citizens of New Westminster, free thought, free food stamps, free university, free rest cures for the mothers of battered babies, free toilets in airports (she picketed outside one for two weeks in support of that cause), free lunch-time concerts for office workers, free tickets home for runaway teenagers. The word "free" ranges wildly and giddily in Greta's consciousness, and often—a special irony—it means something like its opposite since she will go to extraordinary lengths to enforce her concept of freedom.

"Into peace," Greta says, leaning toward me again. "Into a larger peace than I ever knew. And I should know—if anyone does." She is referring, Doug and I know, to the breakdown she suffered in her middle thirties and which she mentions at least once on every occasion we are together.

"But you've only been in the meditation thing for a month," I remind her, playing my role of visiting skeptic.

"You're right," she whispers, and the bones of her small face gleam with alabaster zeal through her unbelievably fragile skin. Such a tiny woman, she is far too small to hold all that latent forcefulness. But her voice is full, chalky with mysticism, rich with caring. "I thought

7

I knew myself before, but I was wrong. I didn't know what real peace was."

"Really?" I ask.

"Charleen, Charleen," Doug says fondly but disapprovingly. "You are the ultimate disbeliever."

"Me? A disbeliever?"

"You. Don't you believe in anything?"

I chew my chicken and think hard. They watch me and wait patiently for an answer. Their concern touches me; I want to please them.

"Friends," I say. "People. I believe in people."

They relax. Smile. Sit back. We sip the last of the wine slowly and fold our red linen napkins with bemused inattention. Doug pays the bill and we rise together.

Arms linked, the three of us stroll down Granby. I walk in the middle as befits my position of erstwhile child. The street is full of people leaving restaurants, buying newspapers, walking dogs. Drunks and lovers lounge in the greyed shadows of buildings, and, though it is eleven o'clock at night, there is a Chinese family, a father, mother and a string of smiling children strolling along ahead of us. We are all melting together in this soft and buzzing electric blaze.

Greta and Doug walk me all the way home. I know they would like me to invite them up for coffee. They are pleased with me tonight, cheered by my declaration of faith and by the warmth of our friendship. They don't want to let me go. I sense their yearning for my straw-matted living room and my blue and white striped coffee mugs, my steaming Nescafé. Their faces turn to me.

But I shake my head. Hold out my hand. "Thank you both for a good evening," I stretch out that little word *good* to make it mean more than it does "I'll see you when I get back from Toronto."

Doug embraces me; Greta kisses my cheek, a crepe

paper grazing. I get out my key and don't turn around again.

❦

My apartment consists of three rooms on the second floor of a narrow, old house. I don't count the kitchen which is no more than a strip of cupboards and a miniature stove in a shuttered off end of the green and white living room. The living room has a serenity which does not in any way reflect my personality; perhaps I am attempting, with these white walls and this cheap, chaste furniture, to impose order and bravery on my life; it takes courage to live with wicker; it takes purity, a false purity in my case, to resist posters, beaded curtains and one more piece of handthrown pottery. There is a small, blue Indian rug on the wall which Watson and I bought for our first apartment. There is a painted plywood cube for a coffee table; Seth made it in grade eight woodworking class. A few books, some greenery on the window sill, a glowing jewel of a cushion which Greta Savage made for me years ago. My friends believe this to be a totally unremarkable room. This is not a room for a poet, they perhaps think, for it lacks even a suggestion of eccentricity or excitement; instead of verve there is a deep-breathing dreaminess, especially in the evening when the one good lamp throws soft-edged shadows halfway up the wall.

There are two bedrooms, a room for Seth and a room for me. That's all we need. His door is closed, but I push it open and in the rippled dark see his humped form under a light blanket. I listen, just as I listened when he was a baby, for the sound of his breathing. He has probably been asleep for hours. His tuba sits on the floor on the tiny hooked rug I made for him years ago. (A blue swan swimming on a pale yellow sea.) I move the tuba beside his dresser, tiptoeing, but there is no need to worry about waking him up. He sleeps deeply, easily, and his ability to sleep is one more point of separation between us, another notch for evolutionary progress. I almost always sleep poorly, jerkily, my nights filled either with hollowed-out insomnia or strings of short, ragged kite-tail dreams that flap and jump in the dark and leave me sad-eyed in the morning, like the worndown women in coffee commercials. Seth's nervous system seems to have been put together by agents other than Watson or me; Watson with his combination of creative energy and lack of talent was predestined to fall apart. And I, suffering from a lack of bravery, must expend all my energies preparing for the next test. And the next. And the next.

Seth. I adore his blunt normalcy and good health. His unspectacular brain. His average height and weight. His willingness to please. His ability to go along with things, not objecting for instance, to staying with Greta and Doug for a week, even though he knows they will stuff him with peanut and raisin casseroles and counsel him endlessly on attaining personal peace. He just smiled when I told him. Smiled and nodded. Sure, sure, he said. And when I told him that Eugene might be going along with me to Toronto, all he said was, great, great. Ah Seth, I do love you. Sleeping there, breathing. Keep puffing your tuba, keep smiling, keep on, and, who knows, you might get out of this unscathed.

❦

There's a whole list of things to be done before I leave for Toronto. First, I must pick up my pay cheque at the university, and this means seeing Doug Savage again after having bid him a final goodbye in front of my apartment last night. Something inside me cringes at the carelessness of this oversight; it is the sort of messy misarrangement I create instinctively. Tag-ends. Clutter. A lack of cleanliness. An inability to end things neatly. What Brother Adam would classify as non-discipline. But there is no question of my not going to pick up the cheque; I need the money.

10

Why in the seven years on the *Journal* have I never thought of having the cheque mailed to me at home or, better yet, sent directly to the bank? Other people make such easy and sensible arrangements without thinking. But from my first month on the *Journal*, Doug has handed me my cheque personally, more often than not with his inked signature still wet on the paper. He pushes it my way off-handedly, avoiding my eyes; sometimes it comes floating loosely on top of a pile of proofs. It is as though a more formal payment might rupture our relationship, might make of my job on the *Journal* something serious and official instead of a part-time piece of noblesse oblige, a pittance for an abandoned woman, a soupçon for the bereft wife of his former friend. Nevertheless the cheque is never late, an acknowledgement that though my position might be undefined, my need for cash is absolute and recurring.

Not that I don't work hard. The *National Botanical Journal* comes out quarterly, and except for selecting the articles which are to appear, I do everything. The *Journal* is a generally dull and uninspired affair with its buff-and-brown cover and the names of the main articles listed on the front. Our next issue is devoted almost entirely to new disease-proof grains with a short piece on "Unusual Alberta Wildflowers" tacked on as a sort of dessert. It is a periodical (it would be too much to call it a magazine) by academics and for academics.

Doug is the nominal editor and I am the only employee. First I edit the manuscripts which is a long, picky, and sensitive tightrope of a job; it is essential not to under-edit since clarity and a moderate level of elegance are desirable, but I must not over-edit and thereby obliterate personal style and perhaps injure the feelings of the submitting authors. (Will he object if I pencil out his "however"? Will he fly into a tantrum when I chop his sentences in two or sometimes three or even four?

Will he mind if I switch the spellings to Canadian standard or rearrange the tangle of his footnotes?) Sometimes I consult Doug.

"You worry too much, Char," is what he usually says, or "Screw the bastard, he's lucky we're going to run his lousy article at all." Doug inherited the editorship of the *Journal* from Watson who abandoned it along with his other responsibilities, and not surprisingly he regards it as a time-consuming stepchild. He is entirely unwilling to worry about the theoretical sensitivities of contributing botanists. But I do; I rarely make a change in an article without anticipating a blast of indignation. In actuality it hardly ever happens, because, for some reason, these unseen scientists are astonishingly submissive to the slash of my red pencil; they quite willingly accept mutilations to their work, the dictates of Charleen Forrest, a thirty-eight-year-old divorcée who knows nothing about botany and who has no training beyond high school unless you count a six-week typing course. Amazing.

After the galley proofs and the layout dummy come the vandykes, these blueprints of the final round, and then another issue is on its way. Time to begin the next. It is relentless but sustaining. Maybe rhythm is all I need to keep me going.

I only work in the mornings since there isn't enough money to pay a full-time employee, and theoretically my afternoons are saved for the writing of poetry, what Doug Savage calls the practice of my craft. Craft. As though one put poetry together from a boxed kit. Not that it matters much what you call it, for it is a fact that in the last two years I've hardly written a line. What once consumed the best of my energies now seems a dull indulgence.

My afternoons just melt away. Sometimes I meet Eugene if he isn't too busy at the office. I shop for groceries, read, worry. I write letters to anyone I can think of, for chief among my diseases is an unwillingness to let friendships die a natural death. I cling, pursuing old friends, dredging up school mates from Scarborough like Sally Cork and Mary Lou Lester. I write to Mary Lou's mother, too, and to her sister in Winnipeg whom I scarcely know. I badger the friends Watson and I once had with my insistent, pressing six pages of hectic persevering scrawl. I even write regularly to a woman named Fay Cousins in northern California who once shared a hundred-mile bus ride with me. And for the last fifteen months I've been writing to Brother Adam, the only correspondent I've ever had who approaches me in scope and endurance.

I cannot let go. It is a kind of game I play in which I pretend, to myself at least, that I, with my paper and envelopes, my pen and my stamps, that I am one of those nice people who care about people. A lovely person. A loving person, a giving person. I dream for myself visions of generosity and kindness. I *care* about Fay Cousin's drinking problem, about Mrs. Lester's ulcerated colon, about Sally's home freezing and Mary Lou's fat braggart of a husband. I *care* about them. At least I want to care.

To my mother I write once a month. And that's hard enough. To my sister Judith perhaps three or four times a year; I would write to Judith more often if I were not so baffled by her lack of neuroses; we had the same childhood, but she somehow survived, and the margin of her survival widens every year so that, though I can talk easily enough to her when I see her, I cannot bear the thought of her reading my letters in the incandescent light of her balanced serenity. Does she understand? Probably not.

And Watson. I never write to Watson. Nor does he

write to me; no one hears from him anymore except Greta who, by trading on a belief that she and Watson are partners in emotional calamity, manages to elicit an occasional note from him. Watson is not cruel; it is only that he is missing one or two of the vital components which happy and normal people possess. Nevertheless, I ache to write to him; just thinking about it makes my fingers want to curl around the words, to smooth the paper. I *long* to write to him. He lives in a commune in Weedham, Ontario, with God only knows who, and all he sends me is child support money. Every month when it comes I examine the handwriting on the cheque, hoping it will contain some kind of declaration, but it is always the same; one hundred and fifty dollars and no cents. Signed, Watson Forrest. That's all.

Sometimes I go for walks in the afternoons and quite often I go all the way to Walkley Street, past the house where Watson and I used to live. We paid exactly $17,900 for that house, and all but one thousand dollars was mortgaged. It is in much better condition than it used to be. The hedges are shaped into startled spheres, and pink and white petunias tumble out of nicely-painted window boxes. There is a new stone patio by the roses, my roses, where I used to park Seth's pram. The curtains are generally drawn in the afternoons as though the owners, an English couple in their fifties I'm told, are anxious about their polished antiques and Chinese carpets. A ginger dachshund yelps from a split cedar pen. An electric lawnmower gleams by the garage. I am unfailingly reassured by these improvements—I rejoice in them, in fact—for I can foresee a time when this house will pass out of our possession altogether, piece by piece replaced so that nothing of the original is left.

❧

At the university, which I reach by a twenty-minute

bus ride, I work in a cubicle of the Natural Science Building. On my door there is a sign which says: 304 Botanical Journal. I have one desk equipped with a manual typewriter, a gunmetal table and matching wastebasket, a peach-coloured filing cabinet with three drawers, two molded plastic chairs and one comfortable, worn, plushy typing chair in bitter green. There are Swedish-type curtains in a subtle bone stripe, by far the best feature of the room, and the walls are painted a glossy café au lait. From the ceiling a fluorescent tube pours faltering institutional light onto my desk. Oddly enough there is no lock on my door. All the other offices on the third floor have locks, but not mine; the lack of a lock and key seems to underscore the valuelessness of what I do. This might be a broom cupboard. Nothing worth guarding here.

This morning when I arrive, Doug is already in the office, bending over the pile of manuscripts on my desk. "Hiya, Char," he says, not bothering to turn around. "I'm just seeing what we should stick in the fall issue."

Though it is only May, we are already beginning to think about the autumn number; we are perpetually leaping across the calendar in six-month strides, so that this job, besides paying only enough to keep me from starving, simultaneously deprives me of a sense of accomplishment. Completion, realization, fulfillment are always half a year away, a point in time which, when finally reached, melts into so much vapour. Now the fall issue is being conceived before the summer has taken shape and before the spring is even back from the printers.

Clearly Doug has been expecting me. Without taking his eyes off the pile of manuscripts, he slides my pay cheque across the desk. I accept it wordlessly, fold it in two lengthwise (I can never remember if it is all right to fold a cheque) and put it in my wallet. The awkward moment passes, and now Doug turns and smiles at me. "Well, are you all set for tomorrow?"

"Almost," I tell him. "Just a few odds and ends to clear up."

"Greta and I thought we'd pick up Seth right from school tomorrow. That okay with you?"

"Oh, no, Doug. Really, that's not necessary at all. He can get a bus."

"No trouble, Char. We'd like to."

"No, that's just too much bother. It's enough that you've offered to have him." I'm playing my game again, protesting, modest, conciliatory, anxious to please.

"For Christ's sake, Charleen, the poor kid will have his suitcase and tuba and everything. We'll pick him up."

"But he's already planned to come out to your place by bus. He mentioned it this morning."

"Look, Char," he sighs, "Greta wants it this way. She wants to pick him up. You know how she gets. I promised her we could do it this way."

I nod. When Doug and I are alone together without Greta, our relationship undergoes a radical reshaping. We drop all pretense of Greta's being our friend and equal; instead we conspire to protect her, to smooth her path, to bolster her up, knowing full well that her present tranquility is a fragile growth. If she has made up her mind to pick up Seth from school, it must be done.

"Sure," I tell Doug, "I'll tell him. I'll make sure he understands that you'll be along."

"Ah, Char," he says fondly, "you're an angel."

Endearments. That's another of the ways in which we change when we're alone. Doug calls me angel, sweetheart, love, baby—words he would never use if Greta were with us, words which are really quite meaningless but which allow him to toy with certain possibilities of

16

freedom. For he is just slightly in love with me, so slightly that I would never have recognized it, were it not that I find myself responding with sprightly manifestations of girlishness. I grin at him wickedly across the desk. I say "shit" when the printer is late with the proofs. Sometimes I poke a pencil in my hair, give a little cat-stretch at eleven-thirty, put my stockinged feet on the chair, call him "Bossman" in a throaty, southland drawl, and grumble about the work he loads on me.

"I need a week away from here," I tell him. "I've had it with tubers and pollen. And mangled prose structure."

"I hope you get a chance to relax when you're away, Char," he says searchingly. "You need a chance to get away from here and think."

"Now what exactly do you mean by that?" I demand.

"Nothing, nothing. Just that we all need a break now and then."

"Now don't go backing down, Doug. I want to know why you think I need to get away and think. Just exactly what do you believe I should be thinking about?"

"Well," he hesitates a small, slightly theatrical instant, "to be honest, you might think about where you're headed. Greta and I have been wondering if you weren't, you know, on the wrong track as it were."

"I suppose you must be talking about Eugene?"

"Not just about Eugene, not only that. But, well, what he represents. The whole bag you might say."

"You've only met him once," I say waspishly. "And that was just for a few minutes."

"Now, now, Char, don't go getting defensive."

"What am I supposed to do? I happen to be very fond of Eugene. *Very* fond."

He waves aside my words. "I can tell you aren't all that sure of yourself about where you're going with Eugene."

"How can you be so sure?"

"Do you really want to know?"

"I asked you."

"Because you never talk about his job."

"Aha," I say triumphantly, "I knew that's what was bothering you."

"Be honest, Charleen baby. Doesn't it bother you a bit?"

"It's an honest profession," I declare piously. "My mother, for one, would think it was the height of success."

"But what do you think?"

"What's wrong with it?"

"An orthodontist. Think about it! A guy who stands around all day putting little wires on little kids' teeth. . ."

"Somebody has to do it," I say. My head aches and I feel a desire to squeeze my eyes shut and weep, but I can't betray Eugene so easily. "It's a service," I sum up.

"Some service. Milking the middle class. God! Dispensing ersatz happiness through the pursuit of perfect middle-class teeth."

"Well, he did a good job on Seth."

"Seth! The poor kid. Thrown to the vanity peddlers before he's old enough to protest."

"Look, Doug," I say, shaping the words into hard little rectangles, "it was the bite. Get it? It wasn't to make him beautiful, it was to correct his bite."

"And on your salary?" Doug mutters softly in his puzzled surrogate-father voice. "How any guy could take fifty bucks a month out of your salary and not be second cousin to a crook—"

Should I tell him that Eugene would not take any money after the first twenty-five dollar consultation?

That he steadfastly refused, once even tearing my cheque into little pieces? Better not risk the suggestion that I was a woman willing to sell her body for dental care, that a pathetically self-sacrificing compulsion had driven me to an absurd martyrdom; it wouldn't take Doug more than a minute to reach that kind of interpretation. "Let's just drop the whole subject of Eugene," I say.

"All I'm saying is that it's probably a good thing you're getting away with him for a few days. To sort of see things *in context*." His voice softens. "I'm only thinking of what's best for you, Char."

"Okay, okay," I say, stuffing the manuscripts in a drawer and slamming it shut.

Why is it I inspire such storms of preaching? It's not only Doug Savage; my most casual acquaintances press me with advice. Doug, though, has become a full-time catechizer; great gushes of his energy are channeled into the sorting out of my life. In an obscure way he seems to feel responsible for Watson's defection, as do all the friends Watson and I once had, as if they shared a guilty belief that their presence in our lives may have proved the fatal splinter. Which is nonsense, of course. But Doug seems to feel he must look after me. He invented this job for me as a therapeutic and practical rescue mission, and at the time I was grateful. I still am. But isn't it time he got back to his plants, I want to tell him. Or concentrated a little more on Greta who rocks continuously between birdlike vagary and thorny obsession, between her wish to reconcile and her appetite for separation. Does Doug realize that Greta, after all these years, still smothers Watson with letters? That she is perhaps outdoing herself as Seth's fairy godmother, wishing him well but not knowing how to make an acceptable present of her particular caring magic? She is—why doesn't Doug see it?—she is possibly slipping into darker and wilder delusions than he realizes.

But since kindness is a sort of hobby with me, a skill which I feel compelled to perfect, I try to look at Doug kindly. It is not really his fault, I tell myself, that Doug judges Eugene harshly. It is part of his generation, this bias, my generation too, to see people in terms of their professions. It is, after all, a logical outgrowth of the work ethic; vocation forms the spiritual skin by which we are recognized and rewarded. Doug Savage is a botanist, a specialist in certain forms of short ferns. He is defined by his speciality just as his ferns are defined by their physical properties. His wife Greta is saved from genuine ordinariness by the fact that she is a professional weaver. Doug's curriculum vitae for her would run: Greta Savage, weaver, wife. Her actual weaving is immaterial; it is *being* a weaver which endows her with worth. In the same way he thinks of me pre-eminently as a poet, a kindly classification, since I am more clerk than poet these days. He is able to ignore the lapse of my talent just as he has been able to ignore the presence of Eugene Redding for the last two years.

The Savages' objection to Eugene is, I sometimes suspect, rather lumpily conceived and certainly it is seldom mentioned: silence says it all. For the most part they have chosen to ignore Eugene just as they have ignored my other, briefer liaisons: with Bob the insurance adjuster, with Maynard the dry-cleaning executive, Thomas Brown-Davis the tax lawyer (lawyers are okay but only if they practice labour law or take on prickly civil liberties cases—even then their value may be marked down by a hyphenated name or a preference for handmade shirts.)

At parties Doug Savage always introduces me by saying, this is Charleen Forrest, you know, the poet. Then he disappears leaving me to explain with enormous awkwardness that my last book came out more than three years ago and that, though I still dabble a little, poetry is part of my past now. What I don't bother to explain is that having written away the well of myself, there is nowhere to go. The only other alternative would be to join that corps of half-poets, those woozy would-bes who burble away in private obscurities, the band of poets I've come to think of, in my private lexicon, as "the pome people." They are the ones for whom no experience is too small: brushing their teeth in the morning brings them frothing to epiphany. Sex is their private invention, and they fornicate with a purity which cries out for crystallization. They can be charming; they can be seductive, but long ago I decided to stop writing if I found myself becoming one of them.

Both Doug and Greta fear for the future of Seth, that his straight, white teeth and middle-class amiability may propel him toward the untouchable ranks: public relations, stock brokerage, advertising, or even, given the situation, orthodontics.

And if Doug Savage had been acquainted with Eugene for twenty-five years instead of twenty-five minutes, he would still think of him as Eugene the Orthodontist. Pseudo-scientific, or so Doug believes, cosmetic-oriented, a man who tinkers with the design of nature. A shill for pearly teeth. A charlatan with carpeted waiting room, expensive machinery and golf-club manners. Doug sees the already-suspect profession of orthodontia as being coupled with a lack of creativity or discovery; if only he were a real dentist who dealt with the reality of pain and suffering. Eugene, sadly, is in one of the repair professions, a fact which for Doug places the seal on his insignificance. And worse, as far as the Savages are concerned, Eugene is abundantly rewarded for what he does.

I sigh heavily, suddenly weary, and Doug says, "Don't give a thought to the manuscripts, Char." He nods in the direction of my desk. "They can wait."

"Fine, fine," I say absently. I am thinking of all the things I have to do before leaving. Laundry, packing, phone Eugene, make sure Seth has bus fare for school. And there must be something else. Something I've forgotten. Laundry, packing, phone, bus fare? Something is missing.

The wedding present!

"I never bought a wedding present," I cry out. "I completely forgot about it."

Doug says nothing.

"How could I forget!" I marvel. And then I add, "Do you think there's something Freudian about that? Forgetting to buy my own mother a wedding present?"

He shrugs. Drums his fingers on my desk. He is determinedly nonchalant about my oversight, but I can see by the faint, grey frown on his face that he has stored it carefully away. Something Freudian. Hmmm. Yes.

❧

When my mother wrote from Toronto early in April to tell me that she was planning to remarry, the first thing I thought of was her left breast. No, not her left breast but the place where her left breast had been before the cancer.

What I pictured was a petal of torn flesh, something unimaginably vulnerable like the unspeakable place behind a glass eye or the acutely sensitive and secret skin beneath a fingernail. A pin-point of concentrated shrinking pain. A wound almost metaphysical, pink edged, so tender that a breath or even a thought could break it open.

I haven't seen her since her operation which was two years ago. In fact, I have not seen her for five years. She lives alone in the Scarborough bungalow where my sister and I grew up. What fills her life I cannot imagine; I have never been able to imagine. Plants. Pots of tea. Her pension cheque. The daily paper with the advertised specials. Taking the subway to Eaton's. Her appliquéd shopping bag, maroon and moss green, the wooden handles faintly soiled. Her housecoat (a floral cotton, washable), her reading glasses, and toast cut into triangles. Her kitchen curtains, her waxed linoleum. The decaffeinated coffee which she drinks from thick, chipped cups—the rows and rows of bone china cups and saucers, stamped with violets and bordered with gilt, are preserved in the glass-fronted china cabinet for the by-now entirely hypothetical day when guests of inexpressible elegance arrive unexpectedly to sip coffee and sit in judgement on my mother.

My mother is getting married. I have known for a month now—since her short, awkwardly-phrased letter with its curiously bald declaration, *Mr. Berceau has asked me to marry him*—but the thought still sucks the breath from the floor of my chest. I cannot believe it. I cannot believe it.

And why not? Why this perplexity? Certainly there is nothing improper about it; she has, after all, been a widow for eleven years, since our father, to whom she was married for thirty years, died in his sleep, a heart attack in his sixtieth year. A massive heart attack, the doctor had called it. Massive. I pictured a tidal wave of pressure, a blind wall—darkness crushing him as he lay sleeping beside my mother in the walnut veneer bed. He never woke up. My mother, always a light nervous sleeper, heard only a small sound like someone suppressing a cough and that was all. By the time she had switched on the pink glass bedside lamp with its pleated paper shade, he was gone.

And next week she is getting married again. To someone called Louis Berceau, someone I have never seen or even heard of. On a Friday afternoon at the end of May, she is getting married. And why shouldn't she, a healthy woman of seventy? Why not? Only someone bitterly perverse would object to what the whole world celebrates as a joyous event. But easy abstractions are one thing. It is something else to absorb an event like this into the hurting holes and sockets of real life. I should rejoice. Instead a sucking swamp tugs at me, a hint of Greek tragedy, dark-blooded and massive like the violent seizure of my father's heart. My timid, nervous, implacable mother with her left breast sheared off and her terrible indifference intact, is getting married. It can't be happening, it can't be coming true.

❧

When I leave the office I run for the bus, waving like a crazy woman at the driver, "Wait, wait!" The sun is blinding and I stumble aboard fumbling for a dollar bill and handing it to him.

"That all you got? Nothing smaller?"

"No," breathlessly, "I'm just going to the bank now."

Never apologize, never explain, Brother Adam wrote.

"Okay, okay."

I sink into a seat only to be struck anew by panic: did I drop my pay cheque in my frantic search for change? I grope; there it is, folded in my wallet.

I am perspiring heavily. The weather is more like midsummer than spring, and the air is weighed down with dampness. My blouse clings to me across the back. It is an old blouse, six years old at least, with a collar that sags. There is too much material under the arms suggesting rolls of mottled matronly flesh; I should have thrown it out long ago.

What I should do, I think, is go and get my hair cut. But that would cost at least fifteen dollars, even if I could get an appointment and there isn't much hope of that. Like my sister Judith I have heavy, wiry, wavy hair. Crow black hair. Irish hair, my mother always called it with a hint of contempt. Wild. I've never been able to formulate a plan for it. I'm tall, too, like Judith, but rangier, craggier, more angled than contoured; she is older by three years and beginning to widen slightly. I probably will too.

Yes, I decide, I must get my hair cut. Definitely. Right after I finish at the bank. I pat my purse with the cheque folded inside.

In addition to the cheque I have something else in my purse; a three-by-five card with Brother Adam's address written on it. It is really less a piece of information than a personal note to myself, for Brother Adam's address is firmly engraved on my brain: The Priory, 615 Beach-wood, Toronto. Nevertheless, leaving the office, I scribbled it down on impulse and tucked it in the zippered middle section of my purse. Impulse? Of course not, I admit to the leafing-out trees; and hedges outside the bus window. I shake my head, a smile fanning out across my face; I have planned this from the very day I decided to go to Toronto for my mother's wedding. Not actually planned it; no, nothing so definite as that. The idea formed itself like a clot in the back of my head, gradually knitting itself into a possibility: I could, if I had time, that is, visit Brother Adam.

Perhaps not an actual visit. Just a phone call, just to say hello. This is Charleen Forrest. Remember? From the *Botany Journal.* Yes, it *is* a surprise, well, I just happened to be in Toronto for a few days, sort of a family reunion, and well, I just couldn't come this close and not give you a call when your letters have meant such a lot to me and, and, then what?

Maybe I could drop in. Why not? That would be better, nothing like a direct face-to-face after all. Then I could see just what sort of place the Priory is. I'd wear something decorous, my new dress probably, pants wouldn't do, and I could wear a little kerchief on my head; no, that would be ridiculous. I would ring the bell. Or lift the knocker. A heavy old knocker, probably wrought iron, rusted slightly, ornately carved with religious symbols. A tiny, frocked figure would eventually appear at the door, and I would state my purpose. My name is Charleen Forrest and I am anxious to see Brother Adam for a few minutes. If he can be spared, that is. No, I'm not actually a friend of his, but we correspond. Through letters, you know. For over a year now. And I thought since I was in Toronto anyway on family business that . . . .

Perhaps I should send a little note first. Plain white note paper. Nice small envelope, very maidenly, expressly plain. If I mailed it today it would be there in a day or two. Then I wouldn't have to worry about taking him by surprise. Really much more polite and, well, thoughtful. The sort of thing that lovely, caring people do, the sort of thing *he* might do: Dear Brother Adam, I know how busy you are with your grass research and spiritual studies and so on, but I wondered if you could spare a few minutes to see me. I'm going to be in Toronto for a few days visiting my family, and there are so many things I'd like to talk to you about, and some things are hard for me to write about. Your letters have meant so much to me—much more than I can tell you—as I have no one I can really talk to, Brother Adam, no one in the world.

❦

At Mr. Mario's Beauty Box the eyes of the receptionist transfix me. Green-hooded, beetle bright, too close together, riding above a sharp little nose like glued-on ornaments from a souvenir shop.

"I don't know if we can fit you in today," her voice clinks away uncaringly. "What about tomorrow at three?"

"I have to go out of town," I stutter. Am I pleading? Am I giving way to my tendency to be obsequious? I firm up my voice, "It has to be today."

"Well," she says tapping a pencil on the appointment book—and already I can see she is going to work me in— "Mr. Mario himself is free in twenty minutes. If you only need a cut, that is,"

"That's all I need," I chant gratefully, "just a cut, just a simple cut."

She stands up suddenly, reaches across the kidney-shaped desk and tugs a hank of my hair. "About three inches?" she demands.

Three inches off? Three inches left on? What?

"Three inches?" she asks again, more sharply this time.

"Yes, yes, three inches, that would be fine."

I have never been to Mr. Mario's before. In fact, I avoid beauty salons almost entirely except for the occasional cut and one or two disastrous hair-straightening sessions in the days when Watson was trying to transform me into a flower child. Mr. Mario's place shimmers with pinkish light. Light spills in through the shirred Austrian curtains and twinkles off the plastic chandeliers. Little bulbs blaze around the mirrors reminding me of movie stars' dressing rooms. Pink hair dryers buzz and the air conditioners churn. The wet, white sunlight of the street is miles away. I wait for Mr. Mario in a slippery vinyl chair, suddenly struck with the fear that this rosy elegance might hint at undreamt of prices. Much more than fifteen dollars, maybe even eighteen. Or as much as twenty. Twenty dollars for a hair cut, am I crazy? I turn to the kidney desk in panic, but the receptionist eyes me coldly, leanly. "Now," she says.

Mr. Mario marches me to a basin, thoroughly, roughly, drenches my hair and neck, and then he seats me in front of his mirror. For a moment I am reassured by his relative maturity; he has a mid-life shadow of fat under his chin, and his fingers are competently plump and strong. Taking hold of my hair at both sides he pulls it straight out and regards my image in the mirror. Together we stare in disbelief: such Irish coarseness, such obscene length, such unspeakable heaviness.

"What did you have in mind?" he inquires sleepily.

"I don't know," I gasp. "Something different. Just go ahead and cut."

"Okay," he yawns and stepping back he examines me from another angle. "Okay."

The sight of the razor raises new fears—where did I hear that razor cuts are more haute than scissor cuts? This might even cost—I feel faint at the thought—as much as twenty-three dollars. And then I'll have to tip him. Another dollar. God, god.

My hair begins to fall to the floor, and without a hint of delicacy he kicks it to one side where it is almost immediately swept up by a girl in a green uniform. Too late now.

He combs, sections, and clips silently and steadily, his lips curled inward with concentration. "Coarse," he says finally, breaking the silence.

"Yes," I confess, "it runs in the family."

"Italian?" he asks with a flicker of interest.

"No. Half Irish, half Scottish."

"Yeah?" His interest evaporates.

To my right a small shrunken woman of enormous old age sits swathed in a plastic cape; her wisps of hair are briskly sectioned for a permanent, and the pink scalp shows through like intersecting streets. One by one I watch the tight plastic rollers being wound and pinned to the bony scalp. I imagine the ammonia burning through her thin, pink skin, aching. Why does she do this to herself? Her chin wobbles like a walnut as though a scream is gathering there. Her lips move, but she says nothing.

On the other side of me a vigorous woman of about fifty bends forward and lights a cigarette while her rollers are removed by the slimmest of boys in striped purple jeans. "Yesterday," she says, blowing out puffed clouds of smoke, "I went all the way to the fish market for some red snapper."

"For what?" the boy asks, leaning toward her.

"Red snapper. It's a fish. And ex-pen-sive! But I was in the mood for a splurge. Well, I cooked it in a little butter. Then you cover it, you know, and leave it just on simmer. Not too long, say about ten minutes."

"Ten minutes," he murmurs back-combing her gunmetal shrub.

"Ten minutes. Then just a little lemon, you know, cut in a wedge to squeeze. And my husband said to me, you know, you could serve this to the P.M. if he happened to drop by."

"He liked it, eh?"

"So he said, so he said, and he's a hard man to please. Tonight I'm going to do lamb chops. You like lamb?"

"Not too much."

"It's all in how you do it. Most people don't get all the fat out, and with lamb you've got to get all the fat out. But do you know what really makes it?"

"What?" he listens. I listen. Even Mr. Mario seems to listen.

"After you brown it really well, you add just a sniff of white wine."

"White wine?" The striped-pants boy seems a little disappointed.

"You don't have to use the expensive stuff. Why waste good booze in cooking. Just the ordinary poison will do you."

"Do you want to have a little hairspray?"

"Just a little. My husband says it's bad for the lungs. Did you know that?"

"Maybe."

"No, it's true. The whole atmosphere's being destroyed by spray cans. But just a little. It's awfully humid out. And I've got to pick up the lamb chops. That husband of mine.

Husband. Strange word. Medieval. Husbandry, husband your flocks; keep, guard, preserve, watch over.

"Bitch," Mr. Mario whispers lazily in my ear as she leaves.

I say nothing, only smile, obscurely gratified that I have somehow gained his favour. He cups my head with his hands, turning it slightly, then begins cutting again, slowly, slowly, alternating between razor, scissors, clippers; razor, scissors, clippers. Cautious as a surgeon.

"Hold still now," he hisses. "The back of the neck is the most important."

I begin to feel sick. Could this possibly cost as much as twenty-five dollars? In New York hair cuts cost up to forty dollars—where did I read that? Mr. Kenneth or something. But this is Vancouver. Still with inflation and everything, twenty-five dollars is not impossible. Twenty-five dollars! Stop cutting, I want to cry out. That's enough. Stop.

Then he is going all over my head with an electric blower and a little round brush, catching my hair from underneath and drawing it out into rounds of dark fur. Turning, rolling, curving. Stop, stop.

At last. Flick, flick with the brush. Off with the towel.

A puff of spray. I stagger to the kidney desk.

He follows me, drowsy-eyed.

Now.

"How much?" my mouth moves.

"Fifteen dollars," he drawls.

I pull out the bills. Blindly stuff an extra dollar in the pocket of his smock. Run for the door. And in the dancing, white heat I see myself blurred across the window. Or is it me?

Oh, Mr. Mario, Mr. Mario. Always, always, always I've wanted to look like this. Soft, shaped, feathered into a new existence. Me.

My lips perform the smallest of smiles. My neck turns a fraction of an inch. My legs stretch long and cool and slow. What's the hurry. Slowly, slowly, I walk home.

❧

Greta telephones to say good-bye. "Is it true," she asks, "is it true what Doug says? That Eugene What's-his-name is going with you?"

I picture her holding the phone in an attitude of anxious, frowning disbelief, her crow's-feet deepening. (Greta's crow's-feet reach all the way to her soul.)

"Yes," I tell her briskly. "Yes, Eugene happened to have a convention in Toronto at the same time. Wasn't that lucky?"

"A dentists' convention," Greta says sadly, dully.

I want to comfort her. Poor Greta with her Gestalt therapy, her psychodrama, her awareness clinic, her encounter group, her trauma team, her megavitamin treatment and now her obsession with meditation. All she needs is just enough psychic epoxy to keep her from slipping apart. Can't I summon a few words to reassure her? Is my heart so hard that I can't give her those few words?

"Look Greta," I say, "thanks for phoning, but I've got to run. Seth just got in from band practice and I've got a million things to do."

"Seth," I turn to him.

"Yes."

"You have the phone number in Toronto? If anything goes wrong?"

"It's on top of the list you gave me."

"Well, look, Seth, if you lose it, just on the wild chance that you might lose it, you can ask the Savages. I gave it to Doug too. You never know."

"Okay."

"And you've got enough money?"

"Sure."

"Positive?"

"All I need is busfare and milk money."

"You might have an emergency."

"I've got plenty."

"Just to make sure, you'd better take this extra five."

"You keep it, you'll need it."

"I've got lots. Your father's cheque came yesterday. And I got paid today. I'm rich for once. You take it."

He pokes it in his back pocket. "I'll take it but I won't need it."

"I wish you were coming. I hate leaving you here like this."

"It's okay," he smiles across at me. "Anyway, there's band practice every day this week."

"At least we'll be back for the concert. Did you get the tickets?"

"Yeah."

"For Eugene too? And his kids?"

"Yeah. In my wallet. Want me to hang on to them 'til Saturday night?"

"Maybe you'd better, the way I lose things. Anyway, I hope everything goes O.K. here."

"Why wouldn't it?"

"It's just that Doug and Greta can be a little . . . well . . . you know."

"Uhuh."

"A little too much."

"I know."

"Just tune them out, Seth. If they start getting to you."

"Okay."

"You'll be ready after school? When they pick you up?"

"I'll be ready."

"And you won't forget your suitcase?"

"No."

"There are clean socks for every day. And I put in your Lions T-shirt in case it stays hot like this."

"Thanks."

"And your retainer is in a plastic bag under your pajamas."

"Okay."

"Your toothbrush. What about your toothbrush?"

"I'll put it in tomorrow morning."

"Don't forget."

"I won't."

"I sound like a clucking hen. I know I sound like an old hen."

"No, you don't."

"It's just that I'm sort of nervous, I guess. All the rushing around and the whole idea of Grandma,"—I say the word Grandma with a sliding self-consciousness since Seth cannot even remember seeing his grandmother—"getting married and everything. It's just got me a little more rattled than usual."

"That's okay."

"That's why I'm clucking away at you like this."

"I don't mind," he says smiling.

"You've got a nice smile, you know that?"

"I ought to for eight hundred bucks."

"I don't mean your teeth. I mean you *have* really got a nice smile."

"Thanks. So do you."

"Really?"

"Yeah, sort of."

"I wish you were coming."

"I'll be okay," he says. And then he adds, "And you'll be okay too."

Chapter 2

"There's nothing about myself that I like," I say to Eugene as we lie side by side in our lower berth. Contentment, momentary contentment, has lulled me into confession. "The bottoms of my feet are scaly," I tell him, "and have you ever noticed what big ugly feet I've got? Slabs. And two huge corns. One on each foot. I've had those same corns since I was thirteen."

"Luckily no one dies of corns."

"My big toes are crooked," I continue. "I'd go to see a chiropodist if I weren't so ashamed of my feet. And they're the kind of feet that are always clammy, summer and winter. At least in the winter I can cover them up with shoes. But then as soon as it's warm enough for sandals, hot like it was today, that's when I remember how much I hate my feet."

"Try to sleep, Charleen."

"It's too lurchy on this train to sleep."

There is a pause, and for a moment or two I think Eugene may remind me that it had been my idea to take the train. But he doesn't. His divorce has made him cautious, fearful of anything resembling marital bickering. Instinctively he shuns that almost unconscious coinage which passes between husbands and wives: *I told you it wouldn't work. Remember, this was your big idea. What will you think of next? Didn't I tell you? Not again! Are you going to start in on that? Don't you ever listen when I'm talking to you? Don't you care anymore? Don't you love me?*

"Try to sleep anyway," Eugene says gently.

"I keep meaning to buy a pumice stone for my feet," I tell him. "Do you know something, Eugene—I've been meaning to buy a pumice stone since I was fifteen and read in *Seventeen* that there was such a thing. And now, here I am, thirty-eight. What's the matter with me, I can't even organize my life enough to buy a pumice stone."

"We'll buy you one in Toronto." He is only faintly mocking.

"I would love to have beautiful feet."

"Great."

"It would be a start."

Eugene says nothing but yawns hugely.

"It would be a start," I say again, drifting off. I am wearying of my self-hatred. It's only a tactical diversion anyway, a pale cousin to the ferocious self-inquiry which ransacks me on nights less peaceful than this. This is more reflex than ritual, stuffing for my poor brain, packing for the wound I prefer not to leave open.

But it opens anyway, freshly perceived, when I'm wakened at three A.M. by the long, pliant, complaining train whistle. Somewhere in all that darkness we are bending around an unseen curve. It's cold in the Pullman, and my nightgown is wound across my stomach. Reaching over Eugene and jerking the blind up an inch or two, I admit a bar of blue light into our dim shelf. Moonlight.

Sharp as biblical revelation it informs me of the total unreality of this instant: that I am lying in bed with a man who is not my husband, rolling through mountains of darkness to my mother's marriage. This is not melodrama (though the vocabulary it requires is); this is madness, lunacy, calling into doubt all the surfaces and shadows of my thirty-eight years.

Berth. Birth. My yearning to see things in symbolic form is powerful; it always has been; it is the affliction of the hopelessly, cheerlessly optimistic, this pinning together of facts to find patterns. And it is a compulsion I resist, having long ago discovered it to be a grandiose cheat. The rhythms of life are random and irreducible.

Suddenly I am shivering from head to foot. I would like to wake Eugene for the warmth of his body, but at this moment I can't bear to include him. And besides, his green-pajamaed back slopes away from me at an angle which suggests an exhaustion even greater than my fear.

❦

Both of us, Eugene and I, are secondary victims of separate modern diseases, mid-century maladies hatched by the heartless new social order: Eugene because his wife abandoned him for the Womens' Movement and I, because I married a man who couldn't bear to leave his youth behind.

We are the losers. (Misery loves company, my mother always said.) The hapless rejectees, the jilted partners of people stronger than ourselves. Social residue. Silt. Whatever exists between Eugene and me—and Doug Savage is at least partly accurate when he accuses me of bewilderment—is diminished by the fact that each of us has been cast aside, tossed out like some curious archeological implement whose usefulness is no longer understood. Even our lovemaking is lit with doubt: are we anything more than two cripples holding each other up? Can our passion be more than second-rate? Can anything come from nothing?

"She was always something of a bitch," Eugene said about his wife, Jeri, shortly after I met him, "but at least in the early days she confined her bitchiness to outsiders. Like waiters in restaurants. The first time I took her out to dinner—I'd only known her a week or so then and I wanted to take her somewhere, you know, impressive. To show her that country boys don't necessarily dribble soup out of the corners of their mouths. We went to the Top of the Captain and she sent the rolls back because they were cold."

"No!" I gasped delightedly. "Really?"

"Really. She said that she thought more people should take that kind of responsibility when the service wasn't up to standard. Sort of a battlecry with her."

"And you married her after that! Oh, Eugene, how could you?"

"There's one born every minute, you know."

"What else did she do?" I asked greedily.

"Well, then she got into the consumer thing. That must have started after we'd been married a year or so. She started out by returning groceries."

"Like what?"

"You name it. Once she had a jar of apricot jam with a wasp in it. That was the worst, I guess. She mailed that to Ottawa."

"And what happened?"

"All she got, I think, was a form letter. It was being looked into or something. She took back all kinds of things to the store. Lettuce that was brown in the middle. Coffee if it tasted a bit off. Fungussy oranges from the bottom of the bag. Smashed eggs, bony meat. Once, as a joke, I accused her of deliberately buying rotten stuff so she'd have something to return."

"And . . .?"

"Jeri never did have much sense of humour."

"Why did she do it anyway? Did she really care all that much?"

Eugene shrugged. "I could never figure it out. I mean, even then we weren't all that hard up for cash. She always said it was the principle of the thing. She seemed to be mad at the whole world. And consumerism kind of opened a somewhat legitimate channel to her. God, she could work up a rage. Nothing timid and retiring about Jeri. Funny, at first she had seemed, I don't know, just discerning. Knowledgeable. Discriminating. How the hell was I supposed to know if rolls should be served warm. I'd never even thought about it. We never had rolls at home. Bread maybe, or biscuits, but never rolls. And here was this dish with long, blonde hair knowing all about rolls."

"You're too trusting, Eugene."

"Later it got so every supermarket manager in the greater Vancouver area knew her. Once she tried to get me to return something for her. A box of broken cookies. Gingersnaps. It was raining like a bastard and she was about eight months pregnant with Donny and she wanted me to get the car out of the garage and go give the store manager hell."

"And did you?"

"No. Absolutely not. I told her I just couldn't get that worked up about a few broken cookies. I've never seen anyone cry the way she did that Saturday afternoon. She cried so hard she was sick. And she couldn't stop being sick. She was kind of half kneeling on the bathroom floor with her head on the edge of the toilet. I finally phoned a drugstore for a tranquilizer, and when she heard about that she started all over again. Hadn't I ever heard of thalidomide? Was I trying to mutilate the baby and maybe kill her?"

"Maybe she really was crazy."

He paused, thinking. "Sometimes I used to think so. Now I think she was just plain angry. An angry, angry woman. And probably still is. The only decent thing she's ever done is let me have the two boys for weekends.

How they've survived I don't know. You know, sometimes when she was at her worst I would lie awake for hours and make up dialogue. Daydreams, only mine were at night. Just lay there and dreamed up things for her to say, the things I wanted her to say. I'd invent whole scenes just like movies. I'd have her running in the front door all smiling and her hair falling all around her and she would be saying something like, 'look at these beautiful apples,' and then she'd bite into one of them. Or she might be bending over me in bed, smiling and telling me how she was the most—" he stopped, smiling, "the most *satisfied* woman on the Pacific coast and that for once she was contented."

"She must have been satisfied once in a while," I said knowingly to Eugene.

"I don't know. I can't ever remember her looking really happy until she joined the West Van Consumer Action Group. The night she got elected secretary-treasurer was the horniest night we ever had in eight years of marriage. Of course I was more or less incidental to the whole scene." He drew a breath. "God, I still think of that night with a kind of glow."

"Why did you have to say that?"

"What? About feeling a glow?"

"Yes," I said, for I liked to think Eugene had nothing but the most wretched memories of Jeri. Eugene is the same: he prefers to think of Watson as a pure, black-hearted villain.

"Actually Watson was a psychic disaster," I volunteered helpfully.

"Like Jeri," Eugene said. "Selfish, immature."

"Never should have married anyone."

"She couldn't see past her own dumb self-satisfaction."

"He could be utterly, utterly unfeeling."

"Blind. And biting. Even with the kids."

Thus we reassure ourselves, Eugene and I, by contesting the unworthiness of our former partners. Sometimes we grow shrill in our denunciations; they were shallow, insensitive, childish, pathetic. I match Eugene, horror story for horror story, as we conspire to reduce our two partners to ranting maniacs; if they hadn't walked out on us when they did, they would most assuredly have been committed to an institution, no doubt about it.

In this way we contrive our innocence. We reshape our histories; we have not been abandoned, only misled, and we insist that we now are liberated from the impossible, the unbearable, that we are free. I am happy now, I tell Eugene. He is happy too, he says, happier than he ever was with Jeri.

We cling together. Legs entwined, playing at love, we wake early in the morning (who could sleep with all this racket?) and we lie in our lower berth clinging together like children.

❧

In the dining car we are served breakfast by a serious young man with a raw, new haircut and a glistening red neck. A university student, probably, hired for the summer. Under the eyes of anxious authority his hands tremble slightly as he puts down our glasses of chilled grapefruit juice. His eyes never leave the rims of the glasses and his mouth sags open slightly in concentration. It's only May; by August he'll be performing with the gliding familiar detachment of a professional.

Who dreams up breakfast menus on trains? Someone splendidly elevated and detached from the rushed, sour determinate of instant coffee sloshed onto saucers, the whole crumbly-cupboard, soggy cornflake world. Here fresh haddock is offered, haddock in cream, imagine. With a tiny branch of parsley. Poached eggs exquisitely

41

shivering on circles of toast. Or a bacon omelet. Nested in homefries. Marvellous. Served with a broiled tomato half. The pictorial effect alone is dazzling. English muffins on warmed plates. Yes, please. Honey or raspberry jam? Ahh, both please. Butter, carved into chilly balls on a green glass dish. Coffee brewed to dense perfection and poured from a graceful silvery pot. Well, just one more cup. Eugene smiles across at me.

A tenderness seizes us for a middle-aged man sitting all alone at the next table and, half turning, Eugene and I exchange pleasantries with him. Over third and fourth cups of coffee he talks about how he found happiness by selling his car.

"Suddenly it came to me," he tells us. "I had an ulcer. You know? I'm a worrier, and you know what they say. Finally I said to myself, look, what are you always worrying about? And do you know what it was?"

"What?" I ask. I am always polite, and besides it is part of the burden of my life to pretend that I am a benevolent and caring person. "What were you worrying about?"

"Well," he continues, "I didn't realize it then—it was like a kind of subconscious thing with me—but what I was always thinking about was my car. Like any minute the brake linings were going to need replacing. So I'd be driving along and all the time I'd be listening to some little noise in the engine. My wife used to say I'd get a crick in my neck from bending over listening like that. Every time I heard any knocking in there I'd always automatically think the worst. Like the motor was stripped for sure. Or the carburetor was giving out. I used to have nightmares, honest to God nightmares, about needing four new tires all at once."

"And did it ever happen?" I ask.

"No. That's the thing, it never happened like that. Maybe there would be a dirty sparkplug or some two-bit wiring job, and when they told me at the garage that was all it was, I'd break into a sweat. A cold sweat. Well, finally I couldn't take it anymore. Landed in hospital and I was only forty-three years old. An ulcer. I bled twenty-four hours, they couldn't stop it. I'm telling you, that makes you think, when something like that happens."

"I'll bet," I agree emphatically.

"So to hell with this, I said. I want to live my life, not worry it away."

"So you sold your car?"

"That's exactly what I did. Just called over a second-hand dealer and said, 'Take it away, I never want to set eyes on it again.' And the day I sold it was like a stone was rolled off my shoulders. You know what?" He paused. "I was happier that day than the day when I got my first car."

"And you're really happier now?" I ask earnestly. I'm not feigning kindness anymore, for I collect, among other things, recipes for happiness. "You really are?"

"You're darned right," he said, draining his coffee cup and setting it thoughtfully on the saucer. "So I spend a buck or two on a taxi now and then. And train fares and all the rest. But I've got my health, and what's more important than that? I'm telling you, I didn't know what happiness was."

A prescription for contentment. I think of Greta Savage in Vancouver who, for the moment at least, has found a quiet place to store all her missionary longings. And Brother Adam—what did he write me? The only way to be happy is to have no expectations. How fortunate they are to have found their perfect, definable, tailored-to-fit solutions.

And my mother. My mother who achieved, if not happiness, at least a sort of jealous, truncated satisfaction in perpetually revising and reordering her immediate surroundings. All the time my sister and I were growing up, for at least twenty-five years, the main focus of her life was an eccentric passion for home decoration, an enslavement all the more bizarre because of the humbleness of our suburban bungalow, a brick box on a narrow, sandy lot with a concrete stoop, a green awning, and a clothes line at the back.

Always one of the six small rooms was in the process of being 'done over', so that we never at any one time in all those years lived in a state of completion. Decorating magazines formed almost the only reading matter in our house, and from those pages, which my mother turned with anxious, hungering fingers, she fanned her fanatical energy. She could do anything. Velvet curtains, swagged and bordered by hand for the living room, were cut up a year later to make throw cushions. She was nothing if not resourceful, for the throw cushions were later picked apart and upholstered onto the dining room chairs. End tables were cut down and patiently refinished. Often wallpaper samples were propped up along the mantle of the imitation fireplace for months at a time before a decision was reached. Her options were limited, of course, by our father's modest income (he was a clerk in a screw factory). She saved quarters in a pickle jar for two years in order to buy a fake-crystal ceiling fixture for the hall.

She learned to make the most complicated and sheerest of curtains complete with miles of ruffling. She learned to paint, solder, wallpaper, stain and upholster. Several times she rewebbed and covered the armchairs in the livingroom. Mother. A tall woman with a caved-in, shallow chest; she went about the house wearing an old shirt of my father's over her print house dresses and on her feet, socks and running shoes; her legs, I remember, were a mottled white with clustered purplish, grape-jelly

44

veins at the backs of the knees. Sometimes we would wake up in the morning to find that she was already at work, the dining-room floor covered with drop-cloths, the step ladder set up, and there she tottered, her bush of hair snugged in an "invisible" net, her Scottish jaw set, painting a stenciled cornice around the ceiling. A seashell motif in antique ivory.

Her decorating effects were invariably too heavily baroque. Not that I realized this at the time; what I felt in that house was a curious choking pressure as though the walls were being slowly strangled; we were all smothering in layers and layers of airless drapery and plaster. Over the years she showed a tendency toward progressively darker, richer textures. The pine buffet was transformed to walnut, an effect laboriously achieved with the aid of stain and graining tools. In the tiny front hall under the chandelier hung a great, gilded imitation-Italian mirror bought at an auction. Under it was a 'gossip bench' painted gold. She ran to luxurious ornamental fabrics, velvets and brocades bought as remnants, and the sumptious effects of tassles and draping. "You don't need money," she used to say, "if you have taste."

Taste. Taste was what the neighbours didn't have. Taste and imagination. All they ever did, she scoffed, was open the Eaton's catalogue and order rooms full of mail-order furniture. And if they were short of cash they put up with faded curtains when all they had to do was buy a packet of dye from the chain store. (She herself frequently went on the rampage with dying. Perhaps my great insecurity springs from nothing more serious than the fear that my pink cotton scatter rug might be snatched from me at any minute to reappear later in vivid, startling, foreign purple.) The neighbours didn't know what taste meant, she said, or were too lazy to make any improvements. All they needed was to get busy and roll up their shirt sleeves. "Just look," she often sighed, "look what I've managed to make of this house."

Our bedroom, Judith's and mine, was a vision of contorted femininity. For us she favoured shirred taffeta or dotted swiss, pale chintz or nylon net. I remember one summer morning, perspiration streaming down her face, dark circles staining the arms of her housedress as she knelt on the floor of our stifling bedroom off the kitchen, her lips grim with zeal and full of pins, attaching an intricately ruffled skirt to our dressing table. Once, for wall hangings, she framed squares of black velvet to which she appliquéd (the discovery of appliqué opened a whole new chapter in her life) stylized ballet figures. A McCall's pattern, twenty-five cents plus postage. She made us a bedroom lamp from an old, pink perfume bottle from Woolworth's and covered the shade with white tulle; this was one of her least successful ideas, for the tulle began to smoke one evening while Judith was studying, and our father had to carry it outside to the backyard and spray it with the garden hose. Our mother watched its destruction with a minimum of sorrow, for any sign of wear or tear or obsolescence immediately opened a hole in the house which her furious energies conspired to fill.

Our father: what did he think of it all? He was so silent and laconic a man, so shy, so nervously inarticulate that it was impossible to tell, but he seemed to sense that the compulsive forces of her personality were cosmic manifestations which must not be interfered with; to stop her was to invite danger or disaster. All I can remember is his occasional resigned sigh: "You know your mother and her house," as once again we were plunged into chaos.

While she was working on a room she was in a state of

violent unrest, plagued by insomnia and shocking fits of indigestion. She planned her rooms as carefully as any set designer, bringing into life whole new environments. Finally, as the metamorphosis was nearing completion, she would become almost electrically excited, impatiently dabbing on the last bit of paint, taking the last stitch, and, with breath suspended, unveiling her creation.

Later she would suffer agonies of doubt. Was it in good taste or was there something maybe just a little bit tacky or gawdy about it? That pink vase, was it a little too much accent? Too bright? Too garish a shade? Maybe if she spray-painted it dusty rose, yes. Yes.

No one except a few out-of-town relatives and the occasional neighbour ever witnessed her decorating marvels although she always talked of having something, a tea perhaps—the exact type of entertainment was never decided upon—when she got the whole house organized. Organized! And the telephone on the gilded gossip bench seldom rang; she never used it herself except to phone our father at the screw company to ask him to bring home another half quart of enamel for the kitchen cupboards or to tell him she had a headache from the varnish fumes and could he come straight home after work and get the girls some scrambled eggs for supper, she would just slip off to bed if he didn't mind.

I never doubted that she loved the house more than she loved us. Our father and Judith and I only impeded her progress as she plunged from one room to the next. Our very presence made the rooms untidy; sitting on the new chintz slipcover we pulled the pattern off-centre, and our school books on the sideboard disturbed the balance of her ornaments. Once I chipped the Chinese blue kitchen cupboards with the broom handle, thus necessitating a frantic search through all the hardware stores in

Scarborough for patch-up paint, a search she suddenly abandoned when it was decided that the cupboards should be painted a pale pumpkin to match the striped cafe curtains which she planned to "run up" as soon as she finished gluing on the moulding in the front bedroom.

Suddenly it stopped. Overnight her obsession became a memory, the way she was before she got old. Judith says it was about the time our father died. I think it was a little earlier. It's been years now since she has made even the slightest alteration to the house. All the upholstery is faded, slightly soiled on the arms, and when I was last there five years ago I actually saw a patch of the old Chinese blue paint in the kitchen showing through the pumpkin. And under that? A scratch of pink? Perhaps.

I don't know why she stopped. I must ask her when I see her. Casually mention something like, "Remember how interested you used to be in decorating—why is it you don't do it anymore?"

But of course I won't actually say anything of the kind. These offhand conversations which I always rehearse in my mind before seeing my mother never materialize because, once in her presence, I freeze back to sullen childhood when all such phenomena were accepted without comment. To question would be to injure the delicate springs of impulse and emotion. For an obsession such as the one which ruled my mother's life could only have existed to fill a terrible hurting void; it is the void we must not mention, for, who knows, it may still exist just below the uneasy quaking surface. Quicksand. So easy to get sucked under. Better to walk carefully, to say nothing.

She may have lost her nerve and become, in the end, finally doubtful about what she had once taken to be taste. Perhaps she simply became exhausted. Or the cost of paint and paper may have strained her small pension. It may be that she suddenly realized one day that all her energy was being poured into an unworthy vessel. Or perhaps she was struck with the heart-racking futility of altering mere surfaces and never reaching the heart: her world was immutable, she may have decided. What was the point of trying to change it?

🌿

Because the Vistadome is packed with people, Eugene and I sit side by side in the day coach, I by the window and he in the aisle seat. We are leaving the mountains behind and for an hour we've watched their angles collapse; they are softening and melting into green, elongated hills which, with their hint of cultivation, are mannerly and almost English. Eugene tells me he has never crossed the Rockies by train before.

"Why not?" I ask.

He shrugs; he is a man much given to shrugging, resignation being the principal inheritance of his forty years. "I don't really know."

"How did you get out of Estevan in the first place?" I demand.

"Bus," he says. "I left on a Thursday afternoon and got into Vancouver late on a Friday night. September. It was the first Friday in September, I remember exactly. I'd just turned eighteen."

"Why didn't you take the train?" I ask, wanting details.

"The bus was cheaper," he explains carefully as though I were exceedingly simple. "Probably only a buck or two, but to my folks—" he stops, shrugging again.

"How did you get home for holidays," I ask, "when you were at university?" These questions are necessary, for though Eugene and I have known each other for two years now, there are miles of unknown territory to recover. Thirty-eight years of his life, thirty-six of mine.

"Hitchhiked," he says. "Then in my third year I bought that old, tan Chevvy. I told you about that."

I nod. Eugene's life is chronicled by the different cars he has owned, separated into periods as distinct as the phases of civilization; his stone-age, bronze-age, iron-age. First the Chevvy, a fourth-hand, first love which he restored to humming perfection on lonely, broke, womanless weekends on the street outside his boarding house on west 19th. Then the Volkswagen beetle with only one previous owner; by graduation he had discovered the benefits of good mileage and reliable repair service. With the navy blue Ford Jeri entered his life. The Rambler: Sandy was born and Donnie on the way and what with diaper bags, carbeds, safety seats and economy . . . the Plymouth wagon, good for groceries. Then the Chrysler; orthodontics was beginning to be rewarding, and though Jeri didn't believe in luxury transport (she had a small Sunbeam of her own anyway), the dealer had offered a package Eugene couldn't turn down. "We used it on weekends," he says, "but I never really knew it inside out. Not like with the Chevvy." The Chevvy. He speaks of it tenderly. "She took me back and forth from Estevan to university three times a year and never once let me down." He smiles, stretched with nostalgia. "She was a good girl. A great old girl."

"And you never once flew."

"Christ, no. It was all I could do to buy gas. I never even set foot in a plane until I was twenty-six and Jeri wanted to go to Hawaii for our honeymoon."

Now, years later, he flies routinely as though no other form of transportation exists. When he decided to come with me to Toronto he tried for days to persuade me that we should fly. "It would save time," he pressed, "and you'd have longer with your mother and sister." (An argument which demonstrates how shallowly he knows me after two years, for what matters to me is to shorten the time in Toronto, not lengthen it.) Besides I went by train the other three times—when I brought Seth as a baby to show him off to his grandparents, then when my father died, and five years ago, when I came home to tell my mother, very belatedly, about my divorce. I had always taken the train; the pattern had been set; and besides, I told Eugene, the train was cheaper.

At the mention of expense, Eugene hesitated, and I knew what he was thinking: that he could easily afford the plane fares for both of us, and since he was planning to attend a dental convention in Toronto, he could write off the whole thing as a business expense. How simple life is for those with professions, savings accounts and good tax lawyers. It was, in fact, this very simplicity that I refused; I'm not ready yet to lay myself open to such soft and easy alternatives.

For days we discussed the matter of plane-versus-train, trading small gently reasoned arguments, each of us having lost the taste for full-scale battle, and, at last, Eugene relented, "But," he said, "if we go by train let's at least come home by air. And let's get ourselves a compartment."

"I sat up the other three times," I said, "and it was fine." Actually it hadn't been fine, but I had, on those three previous trips, accepted discomfort as a kind of welcome detached suffering.

"A roomette?" he bargained. "At least a roomette."

In the end we found we had left it too late; by the time we came to an agreement on the roomette, there was nothing left but one Pullman and at that we were lucky to get a lower. I wanted to pay for half the Pullman but backed down when Eugene began to show signs of gen-

uine impatience. But if he had been even a trifle reason-
able I would have preferred to pay my way. Just as I'm
not ready for comfort (since I've done nothing to deserve
it), neither am I ready to give up what remains of my
shattered independence. First it was dinners Eugene
paid for; then Seth's dental care; last spring a holiday for
the two of us in San Francisco; now my Pullman. And
when I went shopping for a new dress for Toronto, he
had wanted to pay for that too.

I look down at the dress which is really quite comfortable for the train, but like most of my purchases it is
proving to be something of a disappointment; a shirt-
dress in tangerine knit which, even though it is supposed to be permapress, creases across the lap. It is
slightly baggy in the hips and a little snug across the top
so that the spaces between the shiny white buttons gap
slightly like little orange mouths. And beneath my soft,
glossy new hair style of forty-eight hours ago the natural,
black, Irish-witch contours are beginning to reassert
themselves.

Still the two of us sitting here could pass for any happily married couple. Eugene, prosperous and healthy in
his chocolate, doubleknit sixty dollar pants and light-
weight, brown, ribbed pullover, and I, his wife ('the little
wife' you could almost say if I weren't so tall) going along
for the ride, a little shopping, a little holiday from the
kids. That is to say, there is nothing grotesque about us.
We are not perhaps a stunning couple; Eugene has a
loose fabric-like face and thin, beige, wooly hair cut too
short. Without being actually overweight, there is a
somewhat loose look around his stomach and hips. And I
have my usual rangy, unconfined awkwardness. Nevertheless we are not in any way identifiable as the victims
of failed marriages. Nothing gives us away, a fact which
seems remarkable to me. Nothing betrays us, nothing

sets us apart. And because I never let go of anything if I can help it, I am still wearing the wedding ring, a band of Mexican worked silver, which Watson gave me when I was eighteen.

Eugene, I'm a little relieved to see, seems to be enjoying the train trip after all. Soon we'll be getting into the prairies, Saskatchewan, the real prairies where he grew up, and he's looking exceptionally thoughtful. It may be that he's thinking about his father again.

By habit he sees almost everything he does through the double lens of his dead father's limitations, and these reflections are necessarily rimmed with regret, for his father, a hard-working farmer on a piece of worthless land, lived a life of unrelieved narrowness. "My father never slept in a Pullman," Eugene may be thinking. "He never made love behind a hairy green curtain going seventy miles an hour through the mountains." "My father never slept in a tent," he had thought when he went camping for the first time at the age of twenty-five. "My father never rode in a Citroen, never had a glass of wine with his dinner, never went to a concert, never rode in a subway, never ate a black olive, never skied down a hill, never read Hemingway. My father never had a hundred dollar bill in his pocket. He never wore a ring on his finger in all his life. He never sat in a sauna and watched the steam rising off his chest. He never tipped a bellhop or smoked a cigar. Or watched a tennis match or slept in a waterbed in a fifty-dollar a day room with colour television. For that matter, he died while people were still wondering if there would ever be such a thing as colour television."

I am right; Eugene *is* thinking about his father. After a minute he begins to tell me how his father introduced him to the mystery of sex. Of course, Eugene explains, it was already too late. He was a boy of thirteen at the time,

and on a farm there are no such mysteries. "But someone must have told my father that he owed me something more. It might even have been my mother. No, on
second thought, I don't think so. I think he just made up
his mind that he should explain everything about sex to
his only son."

"So he had a long chat with you out in the barn?" I
suggest.

"Oh, no. Better than that. Or worse than that, it de-
pends on how you look at it. I mean, he was a man who
didn't really know how to have a long talk. They didn't
talk much at home, neither of them, and I was the only
kid and fairly quiet too. But he must have figured out in
his head that the time had come for sex. It was when we
were at the fair. The same fair we had every year in
town. More of a carnival really, pretty junky, but there
were some farm animals and home preserving and all
that too. We always went, it was the big deal, the three of
us. There wasn't all that much else to do."

"Go on about the sex."

"Well, this particular day when we were standing in
the fairgrounds, he turned to my mother and said that he
was going off with me for a while and we would meet her
later by the cattle judging yard. So off we went."

"Where?"

"To a girlie show."

"No! Really?"

"Really. It was in one of the tents way, way at the end
of the grounds. There was a big sign—'See The Prairie
Lovelies—Only Twenty-five Cents.' "

"The Prairie Lovelies?"

"And under that was another sign. 'Twenty-five cents
extra for the Whole Show'. Only there was a circle
around the W. The Hole Show."

"And did you know what that meant?"

"Christ, yes, I was thirteen. But I didn't want to go in, at least not with my old man. And I don't think he really wanted to either. He just wasn't that kind of guy. I think he figured he owed it to me or something. God only knows."

"And how were the Prairie Lovelies?"

"Well, we went in and stood around this platform and out came these three girls in kind of Arabian Nights costumes. And they started dancing around. Over at one side some guy was playing the accordian."

"Were they any good?"

"Terrible. Not that I'd ever seen any dancing girls before, but even I could tell they were no good. The audience, of course, was all men, farmers mostly, standing around in their overalls. One of the girls was so fat we could hear her huffing and puffing the whole time she was dancing."

"Wasn't it erotic at all?"

"I suppose, in a way, it was. First the veils came off. Then whatever they were wearing on top. Only this was a few years back and they had flower petals on their nipples. And G-strings under their skirts."

"What about the Hole Show?"

"That came after. That was when the accordian player stopped and announced that we'd have to pay an extra quarter for the Hole Show. The Hole Show. I can remember how he smacked his lips when he said it. He passed a plate around, and I guess pretty well everyone stayed for that."

"And . . .?"

"Then two of the girls kind of faded away, and the other one, the fat one, started in with the bumps and grinds and the accordion going faster and faster all the time while she untied the sides of her G-string. It seemed like forever before she got it off. It was so hot in there you wouldn't believe it, and my father and I standing right in the front. Finally, there she was, peeled right down and sort of squatting and turning so everyone could have a chance to see. There sure wasn't much to see, just a blur really. Then she started dancing again, grinding away, and suddenly she leaned over and grabbed my father's hat off his head."

"His hat?"

"A work hat. A blue cloth hat he had with a peak in front. He never went anywhere without that hat, not that I can remember anyway. You just didn't see farmers bareheaded in those days."

"And what did she do with it?"

"First she sort of bent over and started rubbing it up and down her thighs, wiggling away all the while. Everyone was clapping and yelling like mad by then and banging my father on the back. And then she got wilder and wilder and starting rubbing the hat up against her crotch."

"No!"

"Then everyone went crazy and so did she, just rubbing it and rubbing it."

"What did your father do?"

"Just stood there. Paralyzed. Stunned. Remember he was over fifty then. He just stood there with his mouth open. And his hands reaching out for his hat. Finally she took it and kind of swept it under his nose—that was the worst part—and then she banged it on top of his head."

"Oh, Eugene."

"He grabbed hold of it and ripped it off his head. And threw it on the ground and stomped on it. Then he took hold of my arm, hard, and pushed me on out through the whole damned bunch of them. Right out the doorway. Past the next bunch of suckers lining up outside for the next show. God."

"And what did he say? Afterwards?"

"Nothing. Not one damn thing. I didn't either. We just walked fast all the way to the other end of the fairground where my mother was waiting. He walked so fast I had to run to keep up. I wanted to say something, to tell him it was okay, that I didn't mind all that much about the hat thing, but we never said anything, either of us. Not then or ever."

"Ah, Eugene. And that was your sex education."

"I'm almost sure that's what he intended it to be. Because he sure as hell would never have blown two bits just for the fun of it. He never wasted money. There was never any to waste. I think it was all for me. And she blew it for him, the poor old guy, by grabbing his hat. And so did I by not saying anything."

Eugene shakes his head and, looking out the window, remarks flatly, "It seems a long time ago."

We sit quietly. When Eugene talks about his life, it is always with a sorrowing regretful futility as though the thin distances of his childhood could produce nothing better. But for me there is something compelling about his family, a sort of decency which surfaces unconsciously. I see them in prairie gothic terms, stern but devoted, humble but softened by an unquestioned tradition of love. Nevertheless, at the same time, I find myself listening for something more robust and redeeming, a note of valour perhaps; in Eugene's stories he seems deliberately to choose for himself a lesser role. I yearn for him to demonstrate an aptitude for heroism, and I don't know why. I must ask Brother Adam about that—why do I require bravery from Eugene when I don't possess it myself?

I rest my hand in his lap. We are racing past tiny towns raised to significance by brightly painted grain elevators. Beyond them, fields, a sullen sky, a pulsing lip of brightness behind the clouds. Our train, shooting through air, is the slenderest of arrows, a hairline, a jet trail; it cares nothing for the space it splits apart and nothing for us; all we are required to do is sit still and watch it happen.

From Winnipeg I phone Seth. There is only twenty minutes, but luckily the call goes right through. And it's a good connection.

"Hello. Is that you, Doug?"

"Yes. Charleen! Where are you?"

"Winnipeg. We've just got a few minutes, but I thought I'd phone and see how everything was."

"Everything's fine here. We're all getting along fine."

"Is Seth there?" I ask, and suddenly realize that it is two hours earlier on the coast; Seth might be asleep.

But surprisingly Doug says, "Sure he's here. Hang on a minute, Char, and I'll get him."

I hang on for more than a minute, two minutes, unbelievable! Here I am calling long distance. Long distance—I remember how my mother used to say those two words, her voice stricken, worried and worshipful at the same time.

"Hello."

"Seth," I say, "where were you just now?"

"I was just here," he says maddeningly.

"Well, how are you getting along?"

"Fine."

"How come you're up so early on a Saturday?"

"I just woke up now."

"And you're getting along fine?" I ask again.

"Yeah, just fine."

"You sound all out of breath."

"Oh? I guess I'm just surprised to hear from you."

"I had a few minutes in Winnipeg and I thought I'd just make sure everything was okay."

"How are you?"

"Oh, fine. We get in tomorrow night. Aunt Judith will already be there. She'll probably meet us. At least I think so."

Silence from Vancouver.

"Hello, Seth. Can you hear me? Are you there?"

"I'm still here. I can hear fine."

"Good. Well, I'd better go. Just phone me if you need anything, okay?"

"Okay."

"You've got the number?"

"Yeah."

"Well, I guess I'd better say good-bye."

"Good-bye."

❧

Two years ago when Seth started the orthodonture treatment he was advised to give up his tuba temporarily; for the year and a half while the bands were on his teeth he played the double bass. He was good at it; everyone remarked about how quickly he picked it up.

We bought the double bass third-hand through the want ads; we got it cheap because there was no case. It's a big, waxy, humming buzzard of an instrument, and because its bulk so nearly approximates that of a human being, I soon began to think of it as a sort of half-person, a rather chuckly, middle-aged woman, rather like me in fact.

One day Seth forgot to take it to school and he phoned me between classes asking if I could drop it off. I took it on the bus, feeling enormously proud of her polished, nut-brown hippiness, her deep-throated good nature, the way the sun struck off gleaming streaks on her lovely sides. Seth waited for me on the steps outside the school, frowning and a little anxious that I might be late. When he saw me getting off the bus he jumped up and ran to meet me, taking the instrument out of my arms, whirling about with it and kissing the air about its bridge. I can never get that picture out of my mind, how extraordinarily and purely happy he looked at that instant.

But the minute he had the bands off his teeth he went back to playing the tuba. I can't understand it. A tuba is such an awkward machine with its valves and convolutions; it's such an ugly brassy armload, and I don't understand what Seth likes in the choking, grunting noise that comes out of it.

There seems something rather perverse about his preference. He explains that he likes the tuba better because it's his voice that makes the sounds; the double bass has a voice of its own—it's just a question of letting it out, something anyone can do. I don't think he's touched the bass since. It stands, serene as ever, in a corner of his bedroom. He keeps a beach towel draped over it to keep off the dust, but no one loves it anymore.

Sometimes I think there's something symbolic about it, but symbolism is such an impertinence, the sort of thing the "pome people" might contrive. (God knows how easily it's manufactured by those who turn themselves into continuously operating sensitivity machines.) Of course, symbols have their uses. But something—my cramped Scarborough girlhood no doubt—ties me to the heaviness of facts. Tubas and double basses are not symbols but facts, facts which can be—which must be—assimilated like any of the other mysterious facts of existence.

❧

As the train moves closer to Toronto I decide I must warn Eugene a little about my mother. "She's always been a difficult person," I say.

"How do you mean, difficult?"

"Well, to begin with—you'll notice this right away—she's never been what you'd call demonstrative."

"But she must have loved you. You and your sister?"

"It's hard to explain," I say. Hard because she *had* loved us but with an angry, depriving love which, even after all these years, I don't understand. The lye-bite of her private rancour, her bitter shrivelling scoldings. When she scrubbed our faces it was with a single, hurting swipe. When we fell down and scraped our knees and elbows she said, "that will teach you to watch where you're going." Her love, if that's what you call it, was primitive, scalding, shorn of kindness. I can't explain it to Eugene; instead, I give him an example.

"When she brushed our hair in the morning, Judith's and mine, when she brushed our hair . . . ."

"Yes?"

"She yanked it. Hard. It really hurt. She'd catch us in our bedroom, just before we left for school. She'd be holding the brush in her hand. When I think about it I can still feel her yanking my head back."

Eugene listens without comment.

I shrug, afraid I've betrayed a streak of self-pity. "That's just the way she is, and don't ask me why. I don't understand it. So how could you."

❧

I had forgotten about the thousand miles of bush between Winnipeg and Toronto. But here it is. Eugene and I are sitting high up in the Vistadome with nothing but curved glass separating us from turquoise lakes, whorled trees, the torn, reddened sky and, here and there, clumps of Indian cabins. We're sitting close to the front and so high up that we can overlook our whole train from end to end. We seem to vibrate to a different rhythm up here; the side-to-side swaying is gone; from this position we glide on cables of pure ozone. And music pours sweetly out of the chromium walls: Some Enchanted Evening. The hills are alive with the Sound of Music.

Dancing in the Dark. Temptation—a tango—*You came, I was alone, I should have known you were temptation.* Eugene reaches over and takes my hand.

We met two years ago through mutual friends, the Freehorns, at a small dinner party in late May. It had been an utterly respectable occasion, in every way the reverse of my meeting with Watson which had occurred in a run-down neighbourhood drugstore, a meeting which was described in those days as a pick-up. *Watson was someone who picked up people. I was someone who had allowed myself to be picked up; was that what doomed us?*

But the meeting between Eugene and me was impeccably prearranged, although Bea Freehorn assured me before the party that even though she was inviting a single man, I was not to suspect her of matchmaking. "There's nothing that burns me up more than being accused of fixing someone up," she told me over the phone. "But Eugene's a pet, you'll like him. Merv thinks he's terrific."

Merv and Bea are old friends, so old that they date from the days when I was still married to Watson; the four of us, in times which now seem impossibly idyllic, used to take Sunday picnics up to the mountain; I would bring potato salad and a cake and Bea always brought salami and corned beef and sometimes cold chicken. Now they give dinner parties; I've tried to fix the year when they stopped inviting me to dinner and started inviting me to dinner parties. Sometime when Merv was between assistant and associate in the Law School. Or maybe after they moved into the new house, yes, I think that was it. They have a patio overlooking the ocean where Bea likes to serve dinner on tiny lantern-lit tables. She is an accomplished cook, and I would never turn down one of her dinner invitations with or without a suspicion of matchmaking.

"Actually," Bea had confided, "you and Eugene have something in common."

"What?" I asked cautiously.

"You were both married for exactly eight years."

It's hard sometimes to tell when Bea is being serious. I waited for the rough curl of her laughter but heard only earnest confidence. "He's really had a rough time of it. His wife got screwed up with Womens' Lib and just took the two kids one day and moved out. He has the boys on weekends, nice kids, but she won't take a penny from him, so in a way he's lucky. Anyway, he's a nice guy."

Nice. Yes, I could see that right away when I met him. Nice, meaning polite, presentable, moderate, inquiring and almost sloshily good-natured. He arrived a little late with his right hand freshly bandaged and was apologetically unable to shake hands with the Freehorns, the Stevens, the Folkstones, or with me.

"I was cutting off a piece of beef at noon today," he told us sadly. "The whole plate slipped suddenly and there I was with a bloody gash."

"Oh, Eugene," Bea crooned kindly, "did you need stitches?"

"A few," he said bravely. "The whole thing's been so damned stupid."

I was prepared to dislike him. First for so perfectly fulfilling the role of the inept and picturesque bachelor who couldn't make a sandwich without sawing through his hand. And second for being a self-pitying poseur, and now monopolizing the conversation with his idiotic stitches.

"How are you going to be able to work?" Merv asked him conversationally, and, turning to me, he explained that Eugene was an orthodontist and thus required the use of his hands.

Eugene shrugged and smiled somewhat goofily, "I'll take a week off. There's nothing else to do really."

"What about all your appointments?" Gordon Stevens asked.

"I'll have to get Mrs. Ingalls to cancel everything Monday morning."

"What a shame," Bea mourned, "what a rotten shame. But look, Eugene, let Merv get you something to drink. That hand must be painful."

"It *is* a bit," he admitted.

Did I detect a hint of a whine? Was this ridiculous tooth straightener trying to solicit sympathy? If so, I was not prepared to give it. No wonder his wife ditched him, the big baby. I sipped my gin and tonic sullenly.

"Merv says you're a poet," he said to me later, sitting beside me at one of the little tables along with Gord Stevens and Clara Folkstone. I gave him a long look; with enormous difficulty he was eating his stuffed artichoke with his left hand.

"Yes," I said knowing that he was about to tell me he never read poetry.

"I can't pretend to know much about poetry," he said. "Except the usual stuff we had at school."

"That's all right," I said socially. "It's a sort of minority interest. Like lacrosse."

I had dressed for this evening with deliberate déclassé nonchalance, aware that Bea expects me to contribute a faint whiff of bohemia to her parties; I wore a badly-cut gypsy skirt and black satin peasant blouse, both bought at an Anglican Church rummage sale. Fortunately Bea's expectations conform to what I can afford. I had also brought my special party personality, the rough-ribbed humorous persona which I had devised for myself after Watson left me. I earn my invitations and even for an old friend like Bea Freehorn I knew better than to sulk all evening. So I smiled hard at Eugene as Bea brought round the veal fillets.

Encouraged he asked, "What sort of poet are you? I mean, what kind of things do you write about?"

"About the minutiae of existence," I said with mock solemnity.

He looked baffled and, putting down his fork, he leaned over to whisper in my ear. Now, I thought, now he is going to ask me why poetry doesn't rhyme anymore.

But I was wrong; in a very low murmur, so low that I could hardly hear him, he asked if I would mind cutting up his meat for him.

I almost laughed aloud. But something stopped me; perhaps it was the extraordinary humility of the request or the reserve with which he made it. I leaned over, my elbows grazing his chest and, picking up his knife and fork, I began sawing through the pale, pink veal. My arm sliding back and forth touched the top of his wrist. Clara and Gordon smiled and watched at what seemed a great distance. Three, four, five pieces. I kept cutting, my eyes on Eugene's plate, until I had finished. Then I sat back breathless.

For while I was cutting Eugene's meat, a sudden blood-rush of tenderness had swept over me. A maternal echo? I had once cut Seth's meat in just this way. Perhaps someone had once cut up mine—I half remembered. Eugene's helpless right hand wound in beautiful gauze lay on the edge of the table, and it was all I could do to keep from seizing it and holding it to my lips. I wanted to put my arms around him, to cover him with kisses. The brutal knife, the surgical stitches, the vicious wife who had left him and exposed him to all the hurts of the world—I wanted to stroke them away; I wanted to comfort, to sooth, to minister. I wanted—was I crazy?—I wanted to love him.

We're not far from Toronto now. Another hour and we'll be there. It's getting darker; the towns are closer together now and the farmland is falling into round derby-shaped hills. Eugene is holding my hand and with his middle finger he is tracing slow circles on the palm of my hand. Around and around. The Vistadome where we sit is a tube of darkness. Now he is moving his thumb back and forth across the inside of my wrist. Slowly, slowly. I relax, put back my head, half-shut my eyes. The sound-track of *Zorba the Greek* is washing over us. Lighted towns, squared and tidy, flash by. Eugene has slipped a finger between the buttons of my dress and I can feel it sliding on my nylon slip. Then it retreats; he is carefully, quietly undoing one of the buttons. Now his hand is inside. It is spelling out something on my stomach, a sort of code. I smile to myself.

We flash by Weedham, Ontario. Watson. I had forgotten he was so close to Toronto. No more than thirty miles. Not much of a place; the train doesn't even stop.

Eugene's hand is slowly, slowly inching up my slip, gathering the folds of material. It slides easily. There. He's reached the lace hem. Now I can feel his hand on my bare thighs, the inside of my thighs. The music swamps us. I want to say something but nothing comes; my lips move in miniature as though they were preparing tiny, perfect chapel prayers.

He has reached the edge of my nylon elastic and for an instant we seem balanced on the brink—I think for sure he is stopped. We sit so still.

Then I feel his fingers slip quickly under the elastic and move toward darkness, moisture, secrecy. We are covered with darkness, but on the horizon the sky is soft with reflections. I sit still, half-drowning in a stirring helium happiness. The music rises like moisture and presses on the dark windows, and in this way we ride into the city.

Chapter 3

"Well," I whisper to Judith when we are finally alone.

"Well," she answers back, smiling.

It's midnight and we're standing in our slips in our mother's bedroom at the front of the old house in Scarborough. White nylon slips; Judith's is whiter than mine and fits better. Is there something symbolic about that? No, I reject the possibility.

I love Judith. I had forgotten how much I loved her until I saw her standing with her husband Martin and our mother behind the chaste iron gate at Union Station. She and Martin had come from Kingston on the morning train; we would have a few days together before the wedding.

Judith looked larger than I had remembered, or perhaps it was the colour and cut of her floppy, red denim dress. She has even less fashion sense than I, but unlike me she's able to translate her nonchalance into a well-meaning, soft-edged eccentricity which is curiously touching and even rather charming. She's aged a little. I haven't seen her since she and Martin were in Vancouver for a conference three years ago, and since then she's had her fortieth birthday. And her forty-first. Her daughter is eighteen now and her son is almost as old as Seth. I find myself involuntarily listing the areas of erosion: a small but generalized collapse of skin between her nose and mouth, the forked lines like fingers of an upturned hand between her eyes which make her look not querulous, but worried and kindly, a detached dry point madonna. Her eyes are dreamier than I remembered. Our mother used to fret that Judith would ruin her eyes from so much reading as a girl, swallowing Lawrence and Conrad and Dreiser on summer afternoons stretched on a bath towel in our tiny back yard. Her eyes were sharper then, darting and energetic, the sort of eyes you would expect to harden with age, but they now show such softness. Of course, Judith's life has been embalmed in a stately, enviable, suburban calm. She has a husband who loves her, healthy children, a large, airy house in Kingston, not to mention a respectable reputation as a biographer. And most important, she has a seeming immunity to the shared, sour river of our girlhood.

The house is quiet. Our mother with a long, shrunken, remembered sigh has surrendered to us her bedroom. Green moire curtains discoloured in the folds, a forty-watt bulb in the ceiling fixture. And on the walnut veneer bed, a candlewick bedspread, here and there missing some of its fringe. There is a waterfall bureau, circa 1928, on which rests a precisely-angled amber brush and mirror set which has never, as far as I know, been used. This was our father's bedroom too; how completely we have put away that silent, hard-working husband and father. His wages met the payments on this bungalow; his bony frame rested for thirty years on half of this bed, and yet it seems he never existed.

Since there are only three bedrooms in the house, there was really no other way to arrange the sleeping. No one, of course, had counted on Eugene, least of all Eugene himself who would have preferred a downtown hotel room. It is at my perverse last minute insistence that he is staying here in Scarborough.

Why do I need him here? Perhaps because playing the role of pathetic younger-sister-from-the-west places too great a strain on me. Maybe I am anxious to make a final defiant gesture and give rein to my self-destructive urge which relishes awkward situations—such as how to introduce Eugene to my mother. "This is a friend of mine. Eugene Redding."

Friend? But in my mother's narrow lexicon women don't have male friends. They have fathers, husbands and brothers. Her face, meeting Eugene at the station, had dissolved into a splash of open pain. Had I intended to cause such pain? Why hadn't I written ahead to explain about Eugene? But no one voiced these questions. Nevertheless she shook Eugene's hand slowly as if trying to extract some sort of explanation through his finger tips.

"I really don't want to put you out, Mrs. McNinn," Eugene had insisted. "I told Charleen I would be perfectly happy in a hotel."

There followed a small silence which could be measured not by seconds or minutes but by the cold, linear dimension of my mother's hurt feelings.

"I'm sure we can find room for everyone," she said at last, sounding half paralyzed, like someone who had recently suffered a stroke. "Of course," she trailed off defensively, "it's only a small house."

There was, naturally, no possibility of Eugene and me sharing a room. Anxious to please, I suggested sleeping with my mother and putting Eugene in the spare room, but she shuddered visibly at this idea. "I'd never sleep a wink," she said, plainly vexed. "I'm used to sleeping alone."

Another silence as we absorbed the irony of this statement; in less than a week she would be sleeping with a stranger called Louis Berceau.

Finally it was agreed that Martin and Eugene should take the twin beds in our old bedroom off the kitchen.

Judith and I would occupy our mother's double bed, and our mother, perhaps for the first time in her life, would sleep in the old three-quarters bed in the spare room.

"Couldn't I sleep on the chesterfield?" Eugene suggested desperately.

We waited, breathless, for what seemed like the perfect solution. "No," our mother said with finality. "No one on the chesterfield. That won't be necessary."

What Eugene didn't know, what he couldn't possibly guess, was that no one had ever slept on our chesterfield. Never. Years ago our father, exhausted after a day at work, would occasionally stretch out for a minute and close his eyes. She would poke him, gently but relentlessly. "Not here, Bert. Not on the chesterfield." It was as though she saw something threatening in the way he spread himself, something disturbing and vulgar about the posture of ordinary relaxation.

"Not on the chesterfield," she had said, giving us her final terms, and, like children, we accepted her decree. But inwardly I bled for Martin and Eugene in their forced awkward fraternity. I could imagine their inevitable stiff conversation—*All right with you to open the window? Whichever you prefer. Maybe you'd rather have the bed by the closet? You don't mind if I read for a while? Not at all, not at all.*—Strangers, two men in their early forties, shut up from their women in a tiny back bedroom with no more than a foot or two between their beds, and nothing in common in all this world but a bizarre attachment to the McNinn sisters, Charleen and Judith; they might, for that matter and with good reason, be silently questioning that attachment at this very moment. Martin, an easy man, though somewhat remote, would accept the situation, but he could not help minding the separation from Judith. He had even pleaded for the spare room himself. He and Judith wouldn't object to the three-quarters bed, he had said. But our mother, who seemed to feel that her hospitality was being challenged, had insisted on taking the spare room herself.

"Well?" Judith says again from across the room.

"How do you think she looks?" I ask.

That is always our first question when we're together, how is she, how does she look. Our voices dip and swim with the novel rhythm of concern, childrens' concern for a parent.

"Better than I expected," Judith says.

"When did you see her last?"

"A couple of months ago. I came down on the train with the kids for the weekend."

"She's still getting treatment?"

"She goes every month now. But next year it will probably be less. Down to every three months."

"You talked to the doctor?"

"Yes. A couple of times. He thinks she's made a fantastic recovery."

"What about a recurrence?"

"It could happen. That's why they want her to keep coming to the clinic."

"She looks so thin."

"She was always thin, Charleen. You've forgotten."

"Well, then, she looks old."

"She is old. She's seventy."

"She's so pale though."

"Not compared to what she was after the operation."

"How soon after did you see her?"

"A month. She never told me she was even having an operation. Which was odd when you think how she always used to complain about her aches and pains. She never told anyone. She just went."

"I didn't know until you wrote."

"When I heard—the doctor finally phoned and told

me—I came down and spent a week with her. She was feeling fairly strong by then and there was a nurse who came round every day to check up. She never talked about *it*. It. The breast. Just about the hospital and how rude the nurses had been and how thin the blankets were and how they hadn't given her tea with her breakfast. You know how she goes on. But the breast—she never mentioned it."

"Does it hurt do you think?"

"I don't know. She never says."

"What does she wear? I mean, does she have one of those false things?"

"It looks like it to me. What do you think?"

"She looks just the same there. With her dress on anyway."

"Did you ever see her breasts, Charleen? I mean when we were little."

"Never. You remember how she used to dress in the closet all the time. That was why it was so odd when you wrote me about the operation."

"How do you mean, odd?"

"That she had a breast removed. It never seemed real to me. I just never thought of her as someone who had breasts."

"What did she call them?"

"Breasts? I don't know. She must have called them something."

"Not that I can remember."

We sit on the bed thinking. The house is still and through the window screen we can hear a warm wind lapping at the edge of the awning.

"Developed," Judith says at last, "I think she just used the verb form. Like how so-and-so was developing. Or someone else was very, very developed or maybe not developed."

Remembering, I smile. "She always thought Aunt Liddy was too developed. Poor Liddy, she used to say, she's too developed to buy ready-made."

Judith and I laugh together, quietly so no one will hear. This is the way it used to be. Lying in bed at night, laughing.

"Can't you just hear her telling the doctor that she has a lump in one of her developments," I say.

"And he says, sorry to hear that, Mrs. McNinn, but we'll just have to remove half your development."

We laugh again, harder this time, so hard that the bed rocks. Crazy Judith. I put my hand over my mouth but Judith lets out a yelp of the old girlish cackle. Now we are both shaking with laughter, but there is something manic about all this mirth; it occurs to me that we are perilously close to weeping, and for that reason I reach over and switch off the light.

In the dark Judith asks, "Were you absolutely stunned to hear about Louis?"

"Stunned!" I say. "I'm still trying to get used to it. Is that the way you pronounce his name? Looey?"

"Yes. Like Louis the fourteenth, fifteenth, and sixteenth."

"Have you met him?"

"Last time I was down. But just for a minute. He's coming over tomorrow though. To get acquainted with all of us."

"Where on earth did she meet him? I mean, she never goes anywhere."

"At the cancer clinic," Judith says.

"Really?"

"Yes."

"You mean . . ."

"Yes."

"What exactly?"

"You mean what kind of cancer?"

"Yes."

"I'm not sure. That is, she didn't go into details. But he's had three operations."

"Three operations?"

"Amazing, isn't it?"

"Judith. Do you realize—that means he's missing three parts."

"Possibly."

"What," I speak slowly, "do you think they could be?"

"I don't know. But he doesn't look all that sick. At least not the quick look I had at him."

"What *does* he look like, Judith?"

"Thin. Naturally. And I'm not sure but I think he may be a couple of inches shorter than she is."

"Three operations! I can't get over it. What I mean is . . . don't you think . . . I mean, imagine embarking on marriage when you're in that state."

"Maybe they were only minor operations."

"Is he the same age she is?"

"Two years older. He's seventy-two."

"But he was married before. She wrote that—that he had been married before."

"Yes, but I don't know anything about his first wife, when she died or what."

"Where does he live?"

"He has a furnished room. Not so far from here, just a few minutes. But he's giving it up and moving in here. After the wedding."

"After the wedding," I repeat the words.

"Doesn't it sound crazy? *The Wedding*."

"And he's retired. What did he do before he was re-tired?" I reflect suddenly that I'm not so different after all from Doug Savage; what did he do—that was what I had to find out.

"He taught manual training. In a junior high school."

"Manual training?"

"You know, like woodworking. And metalwork. Like when the girls went for cooking and sewing. Remember?"

"And that was his job? That's what he did?"

"Apparently."

"And he lived in Toronto?"

"I think so. He doesn't speak a word of French, in spite of the French name; I asked him. But he used to be a Catholic."

"A Catholic?"

"Uhuh."

"How do you know?"

"She told me. When she told me about the manual training and all that."

"She would never have told me that. She never tells me anything."

"She doesn't tell me much, either," Judith says. "She writes every week, but it's always about the same old thing: the weather and her aches and pains or how much everything costs these days. I had to pump her about Louis."

"I don't think she's ever forgiven me for running away with Watson."

"Oh, Charleen, that was ages ago. I'm sure she never thinks about it anymore."

"The scandal of it all," I say bitterly. "Having all the neighbours think I might be pregnant."

"Charleen, you exaggerate."

"Well, she never tells me anything."

"Actually, there's something she hasn't told me. And I'm dying to know."

I can't see Judith's face in the dark. "What?" I ask.

"If she loves him. If he loves her."

"I suppose they must. At least a little." But I say this doubtfully.

"I'd give anything to know."

"It's your biographical urge coming through."

"It could be. What I want to know is, do they say romantic things like . . . well, like, 'I love you' and all that."

"I can't imagine *her* saying it."

"I can't either. But maybe he does. Anyway, I wish I knew."

"I don't suppose you could ask her?"

"God, no!" Judith says. "She'd have a fit."

"What I'd like to know is *why*."

"Why what?"

"Why she's getting married. It just doesn't make sense. She's comfortable enough. Why on earth does she want to go and get married?"

There is a long pause. Perhaps Judith has fallen asleep, I think. Then I hear her short sigh, and what she says is: "Well, why does anyone get married?"

❧

"What I'd really like," I say into the darkness, "is some coffee."

"So would I," Judith says. "I wonder if she's got any. She mostly drinks tea now."

"Let's look," I say, slipping out of bed.

"We'll wake everyone up."

"Not if we're quiet."

We move down the darkened hall. Judith walks ahead of me in an exaggerated clownish prowl, her knees pulling up through her yellow cotton nightgown in a burlesque mime of caution. The door to the kitchen is shut; she turns the knob slowly so that there is no sound, and we close it behind us with the smallest of clicks, snap on the overhead light and breathe with relief. Judith faces me, her upper teeth pulled down over her lower lip, girlish and conspiratorial.

Here in the kitchen there is a faint smell of roasted meat. Lamb? A fresh breeze blows through the window screen and the mixed scent of dampness and scouring powder rises from the sink. A newspaper, yesterday's, is folded neatly under the step-on garbage can beside the back door so that there will be no rust marks left on the squared linoleum; it has always been like this.

Our room, the bedroom which Judith and I shared as girls, leads off the kitchen; it is the sort of back bedroom which was commonplace in depression bungalows. Eugene and Martin—it excites me a little to think of it—are sleeping there now. Their door, which stands between the refrigerator (a model from the early fifties) and the old cupboard, is shut; Judith and I freeze for a moment in front of it, listening, straining to hear their fused breathing, but all we hear is the stirring of the wind outside the kitchen window. The trees in the back yard are swaying hugely, and I picture their new green buds, not yet fully opened, turning hard and black in the darkness. "It looks like rain," Judith remarks.

I find the jar of instant coffee at once; without thinking my hand finds the right shelf, reaches for the place beside the tea canister where I know it must be. A very small jar, the lid screwed tightly on. Judith boils water in the green enamel kettle and finds the everyday cups, and then we sit facing each other across the little brown formica table.

Suddenly there is nothing to say. We are uneasy; we are guilty invaders in our mother's clean-mopped kitchen; we have disturbed the symmetry of her lightly stocked shelves, have helped ourselves to sugar from her blue earthenware sugar bowl with its two flat-ear handles and its little flowered lid. "Never leave a sugar bowl uncovered," she always said. "You never know when a fly might get in." It is as though she is sitting here with us now, measuring, observing, censoring, as though she is holding us forcibly inside the sudden, unwilled silence we seem to have entered. I try to drink my coffee, but it's too hot.

Judith says at last, a little warily, "Eugene seems nice." It is not a statement; Judith would never make a statement as banal as that; it is a question.

And I answer conversationally. "I wrote you about him, didn't I?"

As always there is a kind of ritual to our dialogue, for of course I know that I have written to Judith about Eugene and she knows it too. I wrote to her long ago telling her I had met Eugene, that he was working on Seth's teeth, that we had taken a holiday together in San Francisco. I can even recall some of the careful phrases I used in my letters to her. She has not suddenly forgotten, not Judith. It is only that she and I see each other so rarely that we are afraid we might misjudge the permitted area of intimacy. It is necessary to prepare the ground a little before we can speak. There is on Judith's side a wish not to weigh too heavily what I might have written off-handedly and perhaps now regret. On my side there is a wish to project nonchalance and laxity, to preserve at least a shadow of that fiction she half-believes me to be, a runaway younger sister, a casual libertine who has the edge on her, but only superficially, as far as worldliness goes. West-coast divorcée, free-wheeling poet, and now a sort of semi-mistress. We talk in careful, mutually drawn circles.

"When exactly did you meet him, Charleen?"

"Two years ago," I tell her, "two years now."

"And?" Judith asks.

"Just that. Two years."

"What about marriage?" she asks suddenly, reck-lessly, apparently tiring of fencing with me.

"I don't know," I tell her.

"He's divorced too?"

"Yes."

"It's all final and everything?"

"Yes. It's not that. Actually he'd like to get married again. I like his two boys and they like me. There's noth-'ng to stop us really."

"But you're not quite sure of him? Is that it?"

"I just can't seem to think straight these days."

"What about Seth? What does he think of Eugene?"

"That's no problem. He likes Eugene. And he gets on great with the two kids. Seth likes everyone."

It's so quiet in the kitchen. The red and white wall clock over the stove says five minutes past two. The re-frigerator whines from its muffled electric heart and a very fine rain blows against the screen over the sink. Ju-dith gets up and shuts the window.

"Seth likes everyone," I say again. To understate is to risk banality, and these words echoing in the silent kitchen sound both trite and untrue. But they are true; he *does* like everyone, a fact which makes me feel—and not for the first time—a little frightened at my own child's open, unquestioning acceptance. Is it natural? Is it perhaps dangerous?

Judith doesn't notice. "That's good," she says. And waits for me to go on.

"I'm just waiting until I'm sure," I tell her. "I'm not rushing this time. I'm going to wait."

How can I tell her what it is I'm waiting for; I hardly know myself. But I feel with the force of absolute, brim-ming certainty that there is something bulky and posi-tive in the future for me, a thing, an event perhaps, which is connected with me in some way, with me,

79

Charleen Forrest. If I were superstitious I might say it was written in the stars, and if I were half as bitter as Judith believes me to be, I might say it is because I deserve something at last. I know it's there. The numbers tell me: I lived in this brick bungalow for eighteen years. Then I was married to Watson Forrest for eight years. Now I have been divorced for twelve. The shapes, the pattern, the order of those random numbers spell out a kind of logic in my brain; they suggest the approach of another era, another way of being. I'm not a mystic but I know it's there, whatever it is.

❧

I tell Judith about Brother Adam.

She is, as I might have expected, skeptical. Though she prizes her tolerance, in actual fact the edges of her life are sealed to exclude the sort of human flotsam which I have always been able to embrace. The title Brother is not definitive enough for Judith; it is loosely and embarrassingly sentimental, hinting at imposed familiarity and chummy handshakes.

"What's it supposed to mean exactly?" she questions. "Is he a priest? Or what?"

"I think so. I'm not sure."

"You mean in all these letters you've written, you've never asked him?"

I pause; it's hard to explain; some things do not yield to simplicity. "That's the sort of question he might consider trivial. Too particularized, if you see what I mean."

"But you think he *might* be a priest?"

"Well, he lives in a place called the Priory."

"Which priory."

"Just 'The Priory'."

"And it's in Toronto?"

"Yes. In the Beaches area."

"Are you going to see him?"

Another pause. "Maybe," I mumble this 'maybe', chewing the side of my cup, trying to conceal the leap of sensation this 'maybe' excites in me.

"But he *is* a botanist?" Judith asks.

"Yes. In a way. Actually, it's hard to tell."

"What do you mean?"

"He seems to know all about plants. And he sent an article to the *Journal*. I more or less assumed that only a botanist would submit an article to a botanical journal."

"What was it about?"

"Grass."

"Grass? Was it any good?"

"Yes. And no. I liked it. But Doug—you remember Doug Savage, you met him in Vancouver when you were there—he thought it was hilarious."

"You mean actually funny?"

"It wasn't funny. He wasn't trying to be funny at all. It was a serious article, passionately serious, in fact. And scientific in a way. It was a sort of sociology of grass, you might say. He has this theory about the importance of grass to human happiness."

"Maybe he's talking about marijuana."

"No. Just ordinary grass. Garden grass. He's trying to prove that where people don't have any grass, just concrete and asphalt and so on, then the whole human condition begins to deteriorate."

"It sounds a little fanciful," Judith's old skepticism again.

"In a way. I don't understand it all, to tell you the truth. But he writes with the most pressing sort of intensity, something much larger than mere eloquence. Anguished. But reflective too. Not like a scientist at all. More like a poet. Or like a philosopher."

"But nevertheless the *Journal* turned it down?"

"Naturally. Doug thought it was just plain crazy."

"And he gave you the job of returning it."

"Yes. I send back all manuscripts we can't use. And usually I do it fairly heartlessly. But with Brother Adam it was different. I couldn't bear to have him think we utterly rejected what he'd written, that we sneered at what he believed in. I mean, that would be like saying no to something that was beautiful. And humiliating someone who was, well, beautiful too. Don't look so exasperated, Judith. I know I sound fatuous."

"Go on. You sent the manuscript back to the Priory?"

"Yes. But instead of the usual rejection card, I enclosed a little note."

"Saying . . .?"

"Oh, just that I'd enjoyed reading the article, at least the parts I understood. I thought I'd better be honest about it. And I said I thought it was a shame we couldn't use an article like that now and then to break the monotony. Everything we print is so detached. You wouldn't believe it, Judith. I should send you an issue. It's inhuman. The prose style sounds factory-made, all glued together with qualifying phrases. And here at last was an article spurting with passion. From someone who really loved grass. To lie on, to walk on, to sit on. Or to smell. Just to touch grass, he feels, has restorative powers."

"Why grass? I mean, why not flowers or fruit or something? Or trees, even? Isn't grass just a little, you know, ordinary? After all, there's a lot of it around. Even these days."

"That's partly why he loves it, I think. The fact that grass is so humble. And no one's ever celebrated grass before."

"Walt Whitman?"

"That was different. That was more of a symbolic passion."

"What happened after you wrote to him?"

"Nothing at first. A month at least, maybe even longer. Then I got a parcel. Delivered to the *Journal* office."

"From Brother Adam."

"Yes. But you'd never guess what was in it."

"Grass."

"Yes."

We both laugh. "It wasn't really grass, of course." I explain. "It was only the stuff to grow it with. There was a sprouting tray. And some earth in a little cloth bag. Lovely earth really, very fine, a kind of sandy-brown colour. It was clean, clean earth. As though he'd dug it up especially and sieved it and prayed over it. And then there was the packet of seeds. Not the commercial kind. His own. He does his own seed culture."

"And a letter?"

"No. No letter. Not even instructions for planting the seeds. Just the return address. Brother Adam, The Priory, 256 Beachview, Toronto."

"How odd not to send a note."

"That's what made it perfect. A gift without words. As though the grass *was* the letter. As though it had a power purer than words."

Judith laughs. "You always were a bit of a mystic, Charleen."

"But what really touched me, I think, was the parcel itself. The way it was wrapped."

"How was it wrapped?"

"Beautifully. I don't mean aesthetically. After all, there's a limit to the power of brown paper and string. But it was so neatly, so handsomely done up." *With such touching precision. The paper, two layers, that crisp, waxy paper, every corner perfect, and the knots were tight and trimmed and symmetrical like the knots in diagrams. And the address was printed in black ink in lovely blocky letters.* "I hated to open it, in a way," I risk telling her.

Opening it I had had the sensation of being touched by another human being; I had felt the impulse behind the wrapping—and the strength of his wish, his inexplicable wish to please me. Me!

Judith smiles and says nothing, but from her amused gaze I see she thinks I am absurd. Nevertheless she's waiting to hear more. My account of Brother Adam cannot really interest her much—though she is currently writing a biography of a nineteenth-century naturalist and is somewhat curious about the scientific impulse—but she listens to me with the alert probing attention which she has perfected.

"At first I thought of planting the grass at the office, but I was worried it would go dry over the weekend. Besides I didn't want to answer any questions about it. Doug Savage has a way of taking things over." *And besides it would have given his imagination something to feed on; he and Greta cherish my eccentricities as though they were rare collectables.*

"Go on."

"So I took the whole thing home on the bus. Seth thought it was a wonderful present, not at all peculiar, just wonderful. And we put in the seeds that same day. There's quite a lot of sun in the living room. At least for Vancouver. Anyway you don't need strong sunlight for grass. One of the things Brother Adam likes about grass is the way it adapts to any condition. It has an almost human resilience. He hates anything rigid and temperamental like those awful rubber plants everyone sticks in corners these days."

"I like rubber plants."

"Anyway grass can put up with almost anything. I have it in a box by the window and it does well there."

I have to hold my tongue to keep from telling Judith

more: the way, for instance, I felt about those first little seeds. That they might be supernatural, seeds sprouted from a fairy tale, empowered with magical properties, that they might produce overnight or even within an hour a species of life-giving, life-preserving grass. How that night I fell asleep thinking of the tiny, brown seeds lying sideways against the clean, pressing earth, swelling from the force of moisture, obeying the intricate commands of their locked-in chromosomes. Better not tell Judith too much; she might, and with reason, accuse me of overreacting to a trifling gift. She, who has never doubted herself, couldn't possibly understand how I could attach such importance to a gift of grass seed or the fact that it placed a burden on me, a responsibility to make the seeds sprout; their failure to germinate would spell betrayal or, worse, it would summarize my fatal inability to sustain any sort of action.

"Was it any good?" Judith asks. "The grass seed, I mean?"

"Within three days," I tell her, making an effort to speak with detachment, "the first, pale green, threadlike points of grass had appeared. I watered them with a sprinkling bottle, the kind Mother used to dampen clothes on the kitchen table. Every morning and again at night. Sometimes Seth took a turn too."

"And then you wrote to thank Brother Adam for the grass and that was the start of your friendship?"

"Actually I made myself wait two weeks before I wrote. I wanted to make sure the grass was going to survive. By the time I wrote, all of it was up. Some of it was over an inch high. And I cut two or three shoots with my manicure scissors and Scotch-taped them to the letter."

Judith smiles dreamily; I have managed, I can see, to delight her. "But what," she asks, "does one do with a box of grass?"

"It's strange, but I've become very fond of it. It's

divinely soft, like human hair almost. And brilliant green from all that water. I have to trim it about once a week with sewing shears. Sometimes I sprinkle on a little fertilizer although Brother Adam says it's not really necessary." *I also like to run my hand over its springy tightly-shaved surface, loving its tufted healthy carpet-thick threads, the way it struggles against the sides of the box, the industry with which it mends itself.*

"And you've been writing to each other ever since?"

"Yes, more or less."

"Often?"

"Every three or four weeks. I'd write more often but I don't want to wear him down." There is also of course, the fact that an instant reply would place Brother Adam in the position of a debtor—and to be in debt to a correspondent is to hold power over a creditor, a power I sensed he would not welcome.

"What do you write about, Charleen?"

I have to think. "It's funny, but we don't write much about ourselves. He's never asked me anything about myself—I like that. And I don't pester him either. He usually writes about what he's feeling at the moment or what he's seeing. Like once he saw a terrible traffic accident from his window. Once he wrote a whole letter about a wren sitting outside on his fire escape."

"A whole letter about a wren on a fire escape!"

"Well, yes, it was more on the metaphysical side."

"And you do the same?"

"Sort of. I don't so much write as compose. It takes me days. I've hardly written any poetry lately. All of it seems to go into those letters, all that old energy. Writing to him is—I don't know how to explain it—but writing those letters has become a new way of seeing."

"Therapeutic," Judith comments shortly, almost dismissively.

"I suppose you could call it that."

"I wish you wrote to me more often."

"I wish you wrote to me too."

"We always say this, don't we?"

"Yes."

"Charleen?"

"What?"

"What does Eugene think of your . . . your relationship with Brother Adam?"

Judith has always been clever. A bright girl in school, a prizewinner at university; now she is referred to in book reviews as a clever writer. But her real cleverness lies not in her insights, but in her uncanny ability to see the missing links, the ellipses, the silences. Like the perfect interviewer she asks the perfect question. "What does Eugene think?" she asks.

Eugene doesn't know, I tell her. He doesn't know Brother Adam even exists.

❦

After a while Judith asks me if I'm feeling hungry. "We could make some toast," she suggests.

I nod, although I'm not so much hungry as emptied out; a late night hollowness gnaws at me, the grey, uneasy anxiety I always feel in this house. The rain is coming down hard now, leaving angry little check marks on the black window, and the house has grown chilly.

In the breadbox we find exactly one-third of a loaf of white, sliced bread. The top of the bag has been folded down carefully in little pleats to preserve freshness. "A penny saved . . ." our mother had always said. Meagreness.

A memory springs into focus: how I once asked for a piece of bread to put out for the birds. "They can look after their own same as we have to," she replied. Ours, then, had been a house without a birdfeeder, a house where saucers of milk were not provided for stray cats. This was a house where implements were neither loaned nor borrowed, where the man who came to clean the furnace was not offered a cheering cup of coffee, where the postman was not presented with a box of fudge at Christmas. (Such generosities belonged only to fairy tales or soap operas.) In this house there was no contribution to the Red Cross nor (what irony) to the Cancer Fund. Meagreness. I had almost forgotten until I saw the bread in the breadbox.

"Maybe we'd better not have any toast after all," Judith says, tightlipped. "She'll be short for breakfast."

Instead we make more coffee, stirring in extra milk and sugar. I turn to Judith and ask if she has bought a wedding gift for our mother.

"Not yet," she says clutching her hair in a gesture of frenzy. "And it isn't because I haven't thought and thought about it."

"I haven't bought anything either," I admit. "Not yet anyway."

"Do you have any idea what she'd like?"

"Not one."

"Why is it," Judith demands, "that it's so hard to buy our own mother a present? It isn't just this damned wedding present either. Every Christmas and birthday I go through the same thing. Ask Martin. Why is it?"

I'm ready with an answer, for this is something about which I've thought long and hard. "Because no matter what we give her, it will be wrong. No matter how much we spend it will be either too much or too little."

"You're right," Judith muses. (I marvel at her serene musing, at her willingness to accept the way our mother is.)

"She's never satisfied," I storm. "Remember when we

were in high school and put our money together one Christmas and bought her that manicure kit. In the pink leather case? It cost six dollars."

"Vaguely," Judith nods. (Fortunate, fortunate Judith; her memories are soft-edged and have no power over her.)

"I'll never, never forget it," I tell her. "We thought it was beautiful with the little orange stick and the little wool buffer and scissors and everything all fitted in. It was lovely. And she was furious with us."

"Why was that?" Judith wonders.

"Don't you remember? She thought we were criticizing her, that we were hinting she needed a manicure. She told us that if we worked as hard as she did we would have ragged fingernails too."

"Really? I'd forgotten that."

"And the things we made at school. For Mother's Day. I made a woven bookmark once. She said it was nice but the colours clashed. It was yellow and purple."

"Well," Judith shrugs, "gratitude was never one of her talents."

"Eugene suggested I give her an Eaton's gift certificate. But you know just what she'd say—people who give money can't be bothered to put any *thought* into a gift."

"That's right," Judith nods. "Remember how Aunt Liddy used to send us a dollar bill for our birthdays, and Mother always said, 'Wouldn't you think with all the time Liddy has that she could go out and buy a proper birthday present.' "

"Poor Aunt Liddy."

"I thought of a new bedspread," Judith says, "but she might think I was hinting that her old one is looking pretty beat up. Which it is."

"And *I* thought of ordering a flowering shrub for the yard, but she would be sure to say that was too impersonal."

"On the other hand," Judith says, "if we were to get her a new dressing gown that would be *too* personal."

"There's no pleasing her."

"Why do we even try?" Judith asks lightly, philosophically. "Why in heaven's name don't we give up trying to please her?"

This is a question for which I have no answer, and so I say nothing. I drink my coffee which is already cold. We're on a psychic treadmill, Judith and I; we can't stop trying to please her. There's no logic to it, only compulsion; even knowing it's impossible to please her, we can't stop ourselves from trying.

❧

I hadn't intended to talk about Watson; my divorce is a subject I've never really discussed with Judith. It should be easy these free-wheeling days to discuss ex-husbands, but it is never easy for me. In spite of the statistics, in spite of the social tolerance, there is nothing in the world so heavy, so leaden, so painfully pressing as love that has failed. I rarely talk about it—I make a point not to talk about it—but somehow Judith and I have got onto the subject.

We've crept back into bed, and shivering under a light blanket, I ask Judith if she minded turning forty.

"Yes," she answers thoughtfully, "but only a little."

"You didn't feel threatened or anything?"

"Not really. Of course, it helps that Martin gets to all the terrible birthdays first."

"But what about Martin? Didn't he mind?"

"I don't know," Judith says, sounding surprised. And then she adds, "But he doesn't *seem* to mind."

"Eugene is forty," I burst out.

There is a pause; Judith doesn't know what to do with this information.

"Is he?" she says politely.

"And he doesn't mind a bit. He insisted we go out and celebrate it. Cake, candles, the works."

"Well, why not?"

"He likes being forty. I think he'd even like to be older. Forty-five, fifty maybe."

"That's nice for him," Judith comments.

"It's a little worrying, don't you think, rushing into old age like that?"

"Maybe his youth wasn't all that marvellous," she suggests.

I think of Jeri and agree.

"Anyway," Judith says, "the saving grace of reaching forty is that most of your friends get there about the same time."

"I suppose that's a comfort."

"It helps."

"Watson is forty-two," I say. "Imagine!"

"That's right," Judith says, "he was about the same age as me."

"It must have killed him turning forty."

"Why do you say that?"

"Remember how he went berserk at thirty? Forty must have been a funeral for him."

"Of course," Judith says slowly, "I never knew Watson very well, but it's hard to believe that a mere birthday could hit anyone so violently."

"It did though. I saw it coming, of course. Even when he was twenty-seven he was starting to get a bit shaky. Once I even heard him lie about his age. He told some people we met, for no reason at all, that he was only twenty-five."

"Strange."

"He seemed to take it into his head that he could go backwards in time if he put enough energy into it. And that was the same year he started hanging around with his students all the time, especially the undergraduates. And talking about the university as 'they.' He even had me go and get my hair straightened so I'd look like one of his students."

"Poor Char," Judith says softly.

Her sympathy is all I need. Now I can't stop myself. "Then he really began to get desperate. The first time I saw him wearing a head band I was actually sick. Literally. I went into the bathroom and was sick. I wouldn't have minded if someone had given him the head band, one of his students maybe, but what killed me was the deliberation of it all, that he woke up one day and decided to go to a store—it was Woolworth's—and buy himself an Indian head band. And then picking it out and paying for it and then slipping it on his head. And looking at himself in the mirror. That's the moment I couldn't live with, the moment he looked in the mirror at his new head band."

Judith sounds puzzled. "Lots of people wore head bands at one time."

"But don't you see, other people sort of drift into it. They don't suddenly make a conscious decision to hold on to their youth by running out and buying some costume accessories."

"And then what happened?" She is right when she says she scarcely knew Watson. She met him only twice and all she knows about the divorce is that Watson suffered a breakdown. A breakdown?

Perhaps not really a breakdown, although that was the term we used at the time, since it was, at least, medically definable. It was Watson's breakdown which made him

a saint to Greta Savage: she saw it as a powerful link between them, as though their mutual lapse from the co-
herent world spelled mystical union, impenetrable by
those of us coarsened by robust mental health.

But what Watson suffered was something infinitely
more shattering than poor Greta: more of a break-up
than a break down. He broke apart. At the age of thirty
he fell apart. Watson broke into a thousand pieces, and
not one of those pieces had any connection with past or
future.

"When he was twenty-nine," I tell Judith, "he decided
we should sell the house so he and Seth and I could walk
across Europe."

"*Walk* across Europe."

"With backpacks and sandals, a sort of gypsy thing.
He had this crazy idea that he could earn enough money
by playing the recorder, you know, in the streets of
Europe."

"Did Watson play the recorder? I didn't realize he was
musical."

"He wasn't. It was another of his delusions. Oh, he
could play all right, about three tunes, and one of them
was 'Merrily We Roll Along.' It was awful. I don't know
where Seth got his musical ability but it wasn't from
Watson."

"How odd."

"Doug Savage says he became totally detached from
reality. In fact everyone we knew told him he was crazy,
but he wouldn't listen. He actually had this image of
himself tootling away in cute Greek villages with all the
fat, red-faced fishermen loving him. I was supposed to
write poems, Joan Baez style, and he would set them to
music. And if this scheme fell through, he wasn't worried. He was into brotherly love—remember love-ins?—

93

and he was convinced that love was a commodity, like cash, that could take us anywhere. All we had to do was project it."

"What do you suppose would have happened if you'd actually gone?" Judith asks.

"I've asked myself that a hundred times. What if I'd said okay, I'll come. What if I'd taken him at his word, bought myself an Indian skirt and a guitar and followed him. At one point, you know, I had almost decided to go."

"Why didn't you then?"

"Two reasons. First, he stopped wanting me to come. By that time he'd already quit the university. Just walked in one day and told Doug Savage he was finished with Establishment values. He used the word 'establishment' all the time as if it was a hairy, yellow dog nipping at his heels. And then, overnight, it seemed I was part of the Establishment too. Wife. Kid. House. We were all part of it. He stopped talking about walking across Europe with us. We just weren't in the picture any longer. For that last year, in fact, I was his wife on sufferance."

"So he left alone?"

"The day after his thirtieth birthday. Which we did not celebrate, needless to say. He must have got up at dawn. Later I reconstructed the whole thing—I used to torture myself with it. He probably wanted to see the sun rise on the first day of his new life. He was like that you know, very big on symbols. I could just picture how he must have stood in the doorway of our house, very theatrical, with the sun coming up over the hedge. And the note he left! It was like the head band, very studied, very deliberate. A big, fat gesture. I tore it up. Oh, Judith, it was so terribly dumb. I've never told anyone about the note. It was just page after page of youth cult hash. Abstractions like freedom and selfhood, you know the thing. I've never had any stomach for words like 'challenge' and 'fulfillment' anyway, but from Watson . . . I could have died. I was so embarrassed for him."

"Oh, Char."

"I tore it up. And I wanted to burn it but of course we didn't have a fireplace in that house. And bonfires are illegal in Vancouver, so I burned all the little pieces in the habachi out in the yard. And all the time I was burning them I thought how he would have relished the symbolism. He hated barbecues. He always thought they were the altars of North America where people gathered to worship big pieces of meat. He was already into vegetarianism, of course. In fact—and that was what I hated most—he was into everything. Name any branch of the counter-culture and Watson had swallowed it whole. Oh, it was all so desperate. And so badly done. Do you know what I mean? If only he had done it . . . gracefully."

For a minute Judith says nothing. Then she says, "You said there were two reasons."

"What do you mean?"

"You said there were two reasons you didn't go with him to Europe. What was the other one?"

"Because," I say with a short, harsh laugh, "because I was afraid of what Mother might think."

"What about Seth?" Judith asks after a long pause.

"What about him?"

"I don't suppose he remembers Watson. He was only three, wasn't he?"

"No, he doesn't remember anything. Not even the house we lived in."

"He must be curious about him. His own father. You'd think he'd want to meet him."

"No, it's funny but he's never mentioned wanting to meet him. But once he told me he was going to write him a letter. He was about ten then, I think, and it was just after the monthly cheque came. Just before he went to sleep he told me he had decided to write a letter."

"And did he?"

"Yes, he did, and he spent a long time on it. I helped him a little. And it really was a nice kid-like letter all about school and sports and hobbies and his favourite TV programs, sort of a pen pal thing."

"And did Watson ever write back?"

"No. Months and months went by and I kept thinking any day it'll come. I figured Watson couldn't be so cruel as not to write to his own son—after all, he *does* drop Greta a line now and then. Finally I said to Seth how strange it was his father hadn't answered his letter. And do you know what he said?"

"What?"

"He just laughed and said, 'I never mailed that letter.'"

"Why not?"

"I asked him why. I asked him two or three times why he hadn't mailed it. But he would never tell me."

❧

Three-fifteen. The luminous dial of Judith's travel clock announces the hour. She is asleep, lying on her side facing the wall with one arm slung awkwardly, almost grotesquely, over her shoulder. I'm jealous of her ability to sleep, but I am also irrationally pained that she has been able to fall asleep just minutes after I have recounted the miserable story of Watson's breakdown.

My breakdown too; that's the part I didn't confess, the part I conceal even from myself except when I am absolutely alone in the middle of the night as I am now. The day Watson left, everything more or less fell apart for me too. The world, which I was just beginning to perceive, was spoiled. Everything ruined, everything scattered.

Scattered like me, the way I'm scattered through this house: in the spare room where my aggrieved mother sleeps her thin, complaining sleep. And here where Judith lies drugged on my wretchedness. And in the silent back bedroom where Eugene dreams of us riding into Toronto on the Vistadome. In Weedham, Ontario, where Watson Forrest lies amidst the welter of his strange compulsions. And in Vancouver where my son Seth—think of it—I have a fifteen year old son who is sleeping safely in a strange glass and cedar bedroom in the corner of the Savages' house.

But it is not three-fifteen in Vancouver. A rib of joy nudges me. No, it is not three-fifteen. In Vancouver it is late evening. There is probably a soft, grey rain falling. It is not even midnight yet. The TV stations are going strong; the late show hasn't even begun. Doug and Greta almost certainly are still awake; they never go to bed until one or two in the morning. Greta likes to read in bed—she is addicted to crime thrillers—and Doug likes to smoke his pipe and listen to Bartok on the record player. True, Seth may be asleep; he is usually in bed fairly early, but it isn't as though this were the middle of the night.

I'll telephone. I can dial direct; I know the number by heart. It's long distance, but I can keep track of the time and leave money to cover the call. My mother will object—the thought of the charge on her monthly bill will be grievous to her—but it will be too late then. I should have thought of phoning earlier, but there's no harm in calling now, not if I go about it quietly. In fact, this is a good time to phone because the Savages are sure to be at home.

The telephone is in the hallway, a black model sitting on my mother's gossip bench, a spindly piece of furniture from the twenties, half way to being a real antique. I need only the light of the tiny table lamp, and I dial as quietly as I can, marvelling at the technology which permits me, by dialing only eleven numbers, to sift through the millions of darkened households across the country and reach, through tiny electronic connections, the only person in the world who is really and truly connected with me.

But in Vancouver no one answers. I hang up, wait five minutes and try again. The phone rings and rings. I can picture it, a bright red wall model in the Savages' birch and copper kitchen. It rings twelve times, twenty times. No one is home. Can they possibly sleep through all this wild ringing? Impossible. No one is home.

Why can't I sleep? Why can't I be calm like Judith, why can't I learn to be brave? Why is my heart thudding like this, why can't I sleep?

Chapter 4

In the morning my mother's bedroom is filled with sunlight. Someone has opened the curtains, and high above the asphalt-shingled roof of the house next door floats an amiable, blue, suburban sky terraced with flat-bottomed clouds, lovely. Shutting my eyes again I tense, waiting for fear to reassume its grip on me, but it doesn't come.

The sun has brought with it a calm perspective, and suddenly I can think of dozens of reasons why Doug and Greta might not have been at home last night. They might, for instance, have had concert tickets; Doug is a music lover and never, if he can help it, misses the symphony. They might have gone to an exhibition at the university and taken Seth along; hadn't I seen a notice about the opening of a pottery show or something like that in the Fine Arts Building? Or they might have gone out for a late dinner. (Greta frequently has days when, maddened by the world's unhappiness, she cannot summon the strength to cook a meal.) Or taken in a movie. Or gone for a stroll on the beach. There were countless possibilities, none of which had occurred to me the night before.

And this morning, waking up, I yawn, stretch, smile to myself. Nine o'clock. There is no reason to hurry. This evening I can phone Vancouver again; if I phone about ten o'clock I will be sure to catch them at home.

I dress lazily, savouring the rumpled feel of the unmade bed, the open suitcases on the floor, the faintly stale bedroomy air. Through the shut door a burr of lowered voices reaches me, my mother's, Martin's, and whose is that other voice? Of course, Eugene's.

A determined indifference is the perfect cure for anxiety. That's what Brother Adam wrote me. I take my time. I unpack and hang up my clothes in my mother's closet, arranging them next to her half dozen dresses—such dresses: limp, round-shouldered, jersey-knit prints, all of them, in off-colours like maroon and avocado, grey and taupe. They give off a sweetish-sourish smell, very faint, a little musty. Beside them my new orange dress appears sharply synthetic and aggressively youthful. I am sorry now I bought it. For today, I decide, I will put on my old beige skirt instead. And a blouse, a dotted brown cotton which is only slightly creased across the yoke.

In the living room I find Martin, hunched on the slip-covered chesterfield with several sections of the Globe and Mail scattered around him. After all these years I scarcely know him. He is an English professor, Renaissance, and as is the case with a good many academics, his essential kindness is somewhat damaged by wit. And a finished reserve. As though he had spent years and years simmering to his present rich sanity, his pot-au-feu pungency. He is a little uneasy with me—I am so brash, so non-Judith—but his uneasiness has never worried me; our present non-relationship has a temporary, transitional quality; at any moment, it seems to me, we will find our way to being friends. For Martin is a man with a talent for friendship, and in this respect I once believed that Watson resembled him, Watson who knew hundreds and hundreds of people, whole colonies of them secreted away in the cities and towns between Toronto and Vancouver. The difference, I later observed, was that for Watson friendship was not a pleasing dispensation of existence but a means, the only means he knew, by which he could be certain of his existence.

"Well," Martin greets me, "I hear you and Judith made a night of it last night."

"We had a lot of catching up to do," I say. "I hope I didn't wear out her ear drums." I add this apologetically, feeling that Martin might begrudge me a night of Judith's companionship while he himself has been relegated to the back bedroom.

But he smiles quite warmly and says, "Why don't you come and spend a week with us after the wedding and really get caught up?"

"I wish I could," I tell him, "but Seth's staying with friends. And there's my job."

"Surely you could take a few days?" he urges.

Does Martin think I have no responsibilities, nothing to nail me down? No life of my own? And what about Eugene? But I sense that his invitation is no more than a rhetorical exercise; cordial, yes, but mechanically issued. Martin grew up in a hospitable, generous Montreal household where the giving and receiving of invitations was routine, as simple as eating, as simple as breathing.

"Where's Judith now?" I ask, looking around.

"She went out for a few groceries."

I nod, remembering the few slices of bread and the half quart of milk in the refrigerator. "Has everyone had breakfast?"

"Everyone but you. Judith thought you'd prefer to get some sleep. Afraid we didn't leave you anything though. She's gone for some more coffee and bread," he looks at his watch, "but she should be back in a few minutes."

In the kitchen my mother stands washing dishes in the sink; Eugene in a well-pressed spring suit stands next to her, drying teacups and valiantly trying to make

101

conversation. Seeing me in the doorway he almost gasps with relief. "Charleen!"

"Well, you had yourself a good sleep," my mother says, not turning around. (Couldn't she even turn around? Does Eugene notice this greeting, this lack of greeting?)

"Yes," I say, determined to remain unruffled. "I thought I'd be lazy today."

She turns around then, carefully assessing me from top to toe, hair, blouse (creased), skirt, stockings, shoes, and says tartly, "Mr. Berceau—Louis I should say—is dropping by this morning to meet you."

"Good," I answer, rather too lightly, "I'm looking forward to meeting him."

"In that case it's too bad you picked this morning to sleep in. Because you haven't had your breakfast and he's coming at ten o'clock. He's always right on time, right on the dot. We all had breakfast at eight o'clock. Toast and coffee. I told Dr. Redding," she nods sharply at Eugene, "that I hoped he wasn't expecting a big breakfast. We never were a bacon and egg house here. I can't eat all that fried food for breakfast anyway. We just have toast and coffee and always have, guests or no guests. But there's no toast for you. We just completely ran out of bread. That's something I never do normally, run out of things. I plan carefully. You remember, Charleen, how I always planned carefully. There's no excuse for waste, I always say. Of course, I didn't know Dr. Redding would be here, you didn't write about him staying here, or I would have bought an extra loaf. Martin always eats at least three pieces of toast. Not that he needs it. I told Judith this morning he should watch his starches. I never have more than one. I've never been a heavy eater, and a good thing with the price of food. Well, we're right out of bread. Martin even ate the heel, not that there's anything wrong with that. Waste not. Then Judith said, never mind, she'd go down to the Red and White. You'd never know the Red and White now. The floor, it's filthy, just filthy, they used to keep it so clean in there; you remember, Charleen, it used to be spotless when the old man was alive. Spotless. And they let people bring their dogs in, and I don't know what. I thought Judith would be back by the time you woke up but she isn't. I don't know what in the world's keeping her. She always was a dawdler, it's only a block away and it shouldn't be crowded at this time of the morning. And here you are up already. Judith thought you'd sleep in until she got back and here you are and there's nothing for breakfast. You should have got up with the rest of us. And here's Dr. Redding wiping dishes, he insisted, and he's in a rush to get downtown. But Judith said the two of you were up half the night talking away. I thought I heard someone up banging around in the kitchen. You and Judith need your sleep, you don't need me to remind you about that, and here you are up to all hours. How do you expect to get your rest when you sit up all night? You've got all day to talk away. The rest of us need our sleep too."

Eugene, rose-stamped teacup in hand, listens stunned. I have to remember that he has come unprepared, that he has never met anyone like my mother, that she has always been like this. Nevertheless I feel an uncontrollable tremour of pity seeing her this morning in her exhausted, chenille dressing gown, white-faced, despairing and horribly aged, her wrists angry red under the lacy suds.

I watch Eugene standing by the sink, slightly stooped, tea towel in hand, looking at once humble and affluent with his well-trimmed, wooly hair and faintly anxious and uncomfortable expression. It isn't difficult for me to imagine the questions taking shape in Eugene's head, questions he would never voice or perhaps even acknowledge as his own. Questions like: Why is Mrs. McNinn angry with Charleen? What has Charleen done? Why don't these two women, mother and daughter, embrace? Why don't they smile at each other? Why doesn't Charleen ask her mother how she's feeling? Why doesn't Mrs. McNinn ask if Charleen slept well?

As I imagine the questions, the answers too spring into being, the answers which Eugene would almost certainly formulate: Mrs. McNinn is angry because she is not in good health; she is possessed of a rather nervous disposition; it is probable that she slept poorly last night. She is, in addition, confused about who I, Eugene Redding, am, and she is somewhat bothered by the fact that she hadn't been expecting an extra guest. She is unused to house guests and is now embarrassed because she has run short of food. But it is nothing serious; it will pass.

I am able to frame these answers because I know Eugene and trust him to find, as he always does, the most charitable explanation, the most kindly interpretation. Kindness, after all, comes to him naturally; he was hatched in its lucky genre and embraces its attributes effortlessly. Gentleness, generosity and compromise are not for him learned skills; they have always been with him, wound up with the invisible genes which determine the wooliness of his hair and the slightly vacant look in his grey eyes. It may, for all I know, have existed in his family for generations. He is not at the frontier as I am.

For me kindness is an alien quality; and like a difficult French verb I must learn it slowly, painfully, and probably imperfectly. It does *not* swim freely in my bloodstream—I have to inject it artificially at the risk of all sorts of unknown factors. It does *not* wake with me in the mornings; every day I have to coax it anew into existence, breathe on it to keep it alive, practice it to keep it in good working order. And most difficult of all, I have to exercise it in such a way that it looks spontaneous and genuine; I have to see that it flows without hesitation as it does from its true practitioners, its lucky heirs who acquire it without laborious seeking, the lucky ones like Eugene.

Louis Berceau arrives precisely at ten o'clock in a small, dark-green Fiat which he parks at the curb in front of the house. When he knocks at the back door, Judith is making fresh coffee, and Eugene has just left by taxi for the dental convention downtown, an extravagance which both shocked and impressed my mother. ("Doesn't he know we have a subway? Well, I know it's pokey, but it's good enough for most people.")

Judith has been mistaken about Louis's height; he is considerably shorter than our mother, perhaps as much as six inches. And he is thin—certainly I had not expected that he would be robust—with enormously wrinkled, whitish-yellow skin; his gnarled peanut face—how humble he looks!—and his thickish, wall-like eyelids make him look like a dwarfed, jaundiced Jesus. This man has had three operations, I chant to myself. Three operations.

Judith puts down the coffee pot, and he takes both her hands in his and presses her warmly, a warmth which takes Judith by surprise; they have met only once before. Then he turns to me and I see him hesitate an instant before speaking. He has a choked and gummy voice— did tumors nest in that plugged up throat?—but friendliness leaks through. "So this is Charleen."

For a man, he has a tiny hand, harshly-formed, dry and papery as though the flesh were about to fall away

105

from the gathered bones. His clothes, too, seem curiously dry, an old, blue suit, far too hot for today, with faintly dusty seams and buttonholes.

Martin comes into the kitchen to be introduced, and with his hearty "How do you do, Mr. Berceau," we all breathe more easily. My mother, like a minor character in a play, has frozen during these introductions, literally flattening herself against the refrigerator door, nervously observing Louis's presentation of himself to the "family."

"I've just made some coffee," Judith announces.

"Exactly what I need," Louis replies from the top of his strangled, phleghm-plugged throat. "I've been up for hours." And with a rattling sigh he sinks down at the kitchen table.

"We could go into the living room," my mother says with the pinched voice she uses when she wants to be genteel.

"The kitchen is fine, Florence," Louis says, breathing rapidly. Florence! Well, what had I expected?

We sit down at the table while my mother finds cups and saucers in the cupboard. There is a moment's silence which I rush to fill; it seems so extraordinarily painful for Louis Berceau to speak that all I can think of is the necessity of sparing him the effort.

"I'm really very happy to meet you," I rattle away inanely. "At first I thought I wasn't going to be able to come. But I managed to get a week off work, and some friends offered to keep an eye on Seth—my son—and I thought, why not?"

Louis stirs his coffee and lifts his eyes in a disarming, skin-pleated smile. Gasping between spaced phrases he manages, "We are so grateful—both of us—your mother and I—that you could come all these—thousands of miles—to be with us—on Friday. We are—we are—" he searches for a word, then with a final burst says, "we are honoured."

Honoured! Honoured? I glance at my mother, take in her tightly shut lips, and look away. Louis is honoured—how touching—but only Louis.

"It was Mr. Berceau's idea," my mother explains sharply, "to have a proper wedding. And invite," she pauses, "the family."

"Well, you see," Louis chokes, "I never . . . never had a family."

"Well, now you do," Judith says with firm cheerfulness. (How easily I can picture her performing at faculty receptions.) "The children, my two kids that is, have exams this week, but they'll be coming on the train Friday in time for the wedding."

"I hope," Louis says, his thick lips cracking puckishly, "that I'll get to know them well in time."

He drinks his coffee with a long, pleasurable slurp, leans back in his chair—such tiny shoulders—quite amazingly relaxed. Again he strains to speak, and we lean forward, Martin, Judith and I, to catch what he says. "Do you mind . . ." he whispers raspily, "if I smoke?"

He puffs contentedly on a Capstan, using, to my astonishment and horror, the rim of my mother's saucer for an ashtray. The smoke curling from his lips and rather oily nostrils makes him look exceptionally ugly. He has always—I feel certain of this—been ugly; he wears his ugliness with such becoming ease, as though it were a creased oilskin, utilitarian and not at all despised. And as he smokes, he talks, a light and general conversation, faintly paternal with a scattering of questions, the sort of conversation which has rarely filled these rooms. I feel myself grow tense at the obvious exertion of his voice, its separate sounds eased out of the creaking wooden machinery of his throat, dry, high-pitched, harshly monotone, a voice pitted with gasped air as though his windpipe is in some dreadful way shredded and out of his control.

Judith and Martin and I attend scrupulously to his questions, making our replies as lengthy as possible in order to relieve him of the torment of speaking. Turning deferentially to Martin, he inquires about his position at the university, and Martin, not quite blushing but almost, tells Louis that he has recently been appointed chairman of his department.

I am startled. Judith has never mentioned Martin's promotion to me; indeed, at that moment, listening to her husband describe the duties of his new office, Judith fidgets, rises, reheats the coffee, even yawns behind a politely raised hand. She has never pretended to be a standard, right-hand wife, but her nonchalance about Martin's success seems excessive, almost indifferent.

Is Martin himself pleased about his promotion? I wonder. It is difficult to tell because, with his academic compulsion toward truth, he outlines for Louis the enormous liabilities of the position, the toll it takes in terms of time, patience and friendship. Never have I heard Martin so expansive, never so carefully expository, and it occurs to me that he is deliberately prolonging his explanation out of an inclination to break through the aura of surrealism which possesses us, to flatten with his burly, workaday facts the sheer unreality of our being gathered here around this particular kitchen table on this particular late May morning.

Louis turns next to Judith—I am becoming accustomed to his dry-roofed rasp—and asks her whether she has read the biography of Lawrence Welk, a question which disappoints me somewhat by its banality. (Already I am investing Louis with wizened, cerebral kindliness.)

No, Judith answers, she hasn't read it but she respects those who discover ways, whatever they may be, of uncovering currents of the extraordinary in even the most ordinary personalities. Actually, Judith protests, she doesn't believe there is such a thing as an ordinary person, at least not when examined from the privileged perspective of the biographer. What consumes her now, she tells Louis, is her investigation into the scientific impulse—no, not impulse, she corrects herself; in the case of scientists, impulse becomes compulsion. Louis nods; his twisted muzzle face registers agreement. Judith continues: science, she says, often drowns men with its overwhelming abstractions, snuffing out human variability and hatching the partly true myth of the cold, clinical man of science. Human whim, human dream if you like, become obscured, and for the biographer, Judith admits, not unhappily, the scientific life is the most complex of all to write about.

Louis questions me next—I wonder if he has rehearsed the pattern of our discussion—asking me if dreams inspire the poems I write. (It is a morning for speeches, each of us taking a turn, except, that is, our mother who sits in one corner of the table, peevishly sipping her coffee and filling the dips and hollows of our phrases with nervous, trailing "yes's" and "well's"). No, I tell Louis, I never write poems inspired by dreams.

"Why not?" he creaks.

I shrug, thinking of the Pome People who treasure their dreams as though they were rare oriental currency blazoned with symbolic stamping. For me dreams are no more than rag-ends caught in a sort of human lint-trap, psychic fluff, the negligible dust of that more precious material, thought. To value one's dreams is to encourage the most debilitating of diseases, subjectivity. (Watson nearly died of that disease; our marriage almost certainly did.) To pretend that dreams are generated whole out of some vast, informing unconsciousness is to imagine a comic-strip beast (alligator, dragon?) slumbering in one's blood. The inner life? I shrug again. The poet has to report on surfaces, on the flower in the crannied wall, on coffee spoons and peaches, a rusted key discovered in the grass. Dreams are like—I think a moment—dreams are like mashed potatoes.

Martin awards me a yelp of laughter. Louis smiles a yellow, fish-gleam smile, and Judith, smiling approval, refills my cup. She is flushed with her own impromptu eloquence and proud of mine. And puzzled too. Is it Louis's questions that have stirred us? Or our desire to make him understand exactly how far we have travelled from this cramped kitchen?

After this it is Louis's turn to speak.

"With your permission," he begins hoarsely, "I would like to invite each of you—you, Judith and you, Charleen—to have lunch with me." He stops; a coughing fit seizes him, shaking his thin shoulders with wrenching violence. We watch helplessly, tensely, listening to the dry, squeezed convulsions of his heaving chest.

"It's just the asthma," our mother tells us calmly, almost flatly, sipping again at her coffee. "It happens all the time."

Three operations *and* asthma!

At last Louis's coughing stops and he pulls out a handkerchief and blows his nose noisily. Half choking, he begins again, explaining how he hopes to get better acquainted with us by taking us in turn, Judith today and me tomorrow, out for a nice, long lunch. (The order, I can only think, is dictated by our relative ages; Judith being older has priority, and I cannot help smiling at the thoroughness of his planning.) When he has finished his arduous invitation, he sits back again, smashes his cigarette in my mother's saucer, and asks "Well?"

Judith—brave, kind, curious Judith—leaning over the table and placing her hand on Louis's amber-stained fingertips, repeats the word Louis used earlier, a word which has never before, as far as I know, been used in this house and which is now being spoken for the second time in a single morning. "I would be honoured," she pronounces.

"In that case," Louis says rising, "I think we should be on our way."

"You mean right now?" Judith stammers.

"I know a nice quiet place," he rasps, "in the country. It'll be after twelve o'clock before we get there."

Turning to me he says, "Tomorrow then, Charleen? We can . . ." he coughs his parched, tenor cough, "we can talk some more about poetry."

Judith, a little bewildered, picks up a sweater and her handbag and they leave by the back door, walking together around the lilac tree at the side of the house. My mother rises at once to place the cups in the sink. Martin returns to his newspaper and I, following him into the living room, watch the two of them move toward the car; Judith is a full head taller than Louis; she seems to lope by his side.

It is very strange watching Louis walk to his car. Louis, sitting in the kitchen and puffing his cigarette, seemed dwarfed and bleached and freakish, like an aged, yellowed monkey, but Louis walking to the car is close to nimbleness; with his lightsome step, his short, little arms swinging cheerfully, and his head tossing as though he were searching out the best possible breath of air, he appears, from the back and from a distance, like a man in his prime.

❧

We have scrambled eggs on toast for lunch, Martin, my mother and I.

In this household, guests have never been frequent: occasionally when we were children my Aunt Liddy, my mother's older sister who lived in the country, would come to spend a day with us. And there was a second cousin of our father, Cousin Hugo, who owned a hardware store, a large, fat man with wiry black hair and curving crusts of dirt beneath his fingernails. And once a neighbour whose wife was in the hospital with pneumonia had been invited for Sunday lunch, an extraordinary gesture which remained for years in my mother's mind as the "time we put ourselves out to help Mr. Eggleston." Always on these occasions when guests were present she would serve scrambled eggs on toast.

Doubtless she considered it a dish both light and elegant. She may have read somewhere that it was the Queen Mother's favourite luncheon dish (she is always reading about the Royal Family). Certainly she is convinced of the superiority of her own scrambled eggs and the manner in which she arranges the triangles of toast (side by side like the sails of a tiny boat), for she always compares, at length, the correctness of her method with the slipshod scrambled eggs she has encountered elsewhere.

"Liddy doesn't put enough milk in hers and I always tell her that makes them rubbery. If you want nice, soft scrambled eggs you have to add a tablespoon of milk for every egg, just a tablespoon, no more, no less. And use an egg beater, not a fork the way most people do. Most people just don't want to bother getting out an egg beater, they're too lazy to wash something extra. They think, who'll notice anyway, what's the difference, but an egg beater makes all the difference, all the difference in the world. Otherwise the yolk and white don't mix the way they should. Liddy always leaves big hunks of white in her scrambled eggs. And she doesn't cut the crusts off her toast. She thinks it's hoity-toity and a waste of bread, but I always save the crusts and dry them in the oven to make bread crumbs out of them afterwards so there's no waste, not a bit; you know I never waste good food; you'll have to admit I never waste anything. Most people won't bother, they won't go to the trouble; they're too lazy; they don't know any better. And I always add the salt before cooking, that makes them hold their shape, not get hard like Liddy's but just, you know, firm. But not pepper, never pepper, never add pepper when you're cooking, let people add their own pepper at the table if that's what they want. Me, I never liked spicy food like what the Italians and French like. And Greeks. Garlic and onions and grease, and I don't know what, just reeking of it on the subway these days, reeking of it; I don't dare turn my head sideways when I go downtown. Toronto isn't the same; not the way it used to be, not the way it was way back."

We eat lunch in the kitchen. Martin is quiet. So am I. Our forks clicking on the plates chill me into a further silence.

"Hmm, delicious," Martin says politely.

"Yes." I agree, forcing my voice into short plumes of enthusiasm, "Really good. So tender."

Afterwards she washes the dishes and I dry. *Always take a clean tea towel for each meal. It may be a little bit extra in the wash but when you think of the filthy tea towels some people use . . . .*

I yearn desperately to talk to her; to say that, despite my foreboding, I have been rather taken with Louis Berceau, that I am immeasurably pleased that he and she have found each other and she will no longer have to endure the loneliness of the ticking clock, the sound of the furnace switching on and off, the daily paper thudding against the door, the calendar weeks wasting, the reminders of time slipping by which must be unbearable for those who are alone. But the words dry in my throat; if only I knew how to begin, if only I could speak to her without shyness, without fear of hurting her. Instead I poke with my tea towel into the spokes of the egg beater.

"Don't bother drying that," she turns to me, taking it out of my hands. "Here," she says, "I always put it in the oven for a little, the pilot light dries it out; the gears are so old, I've had it since just after the war, it was hard to get egg beaters then. Cousin Hugo got it for me from the store. I don't want the gears to rust, they would if I didn't get it good and dry. I've had it so long and it will have to last me until—"

Until what? Until death? Until the end? That is what she means; the words she couldn't say but which she must have recognized or why did she stop so suddenly? I have never thought of the way in which my mother thinks of her own death. No doubt, though, she has a plan; she will do it more neatly, more thoroughly than her sister Liddy, better than the neighbours, more genteely than Cousin Hugo, more timely than our father; no one will laugh at her, no one will look down on her.

Still, it may be that she is a little uncertain: the way she plunges into vigorous silence beside the scoured sink hints at uneasiness, an acknowledgement at least of life's thinned reversal, of the finite nature of husbands and egg beaters and even of one's self.

After lunch Martin carries a kitchen chair out into the backyard (my mother has never owned a piece of lawn furniture) and there in the sunshine he reads a book of critical essays, a recent paperback edition which he opens with a sigh. He is, I suspect, a somewhat reluctant academic, preferring perhaps to while away his time with the small change of newspapers and magazines.

Nevertheless he enjoys the warmth and the serious Sisley sky, finely marbled, gilt-veined, surprisingly large even when viewed from the postage stamp of our tiny, fenced yard.

One-thirty. My mother goes about the house closing the curtains, first the living room and then the three bedrooms. (Much of her life has gone into a struggle against the fading of furniture and curtains and rugs.) Then she goes into the spare bedroom where she slept last night and closes the door. She is going to lie down, she is going to have her rest. She has always, since Judith and I were babies, had a "rest" after lunch. Never a nap, never a sleep, never, oh never, a doze, but a rest. She will remove her laced shoes and her dress, she will button a loosely knit grey and blue cardigan over her slip and she will turn back the bedspread into a neat fan; then she will get into bed, and there she will remain for between an hour and an hour and a half. Sometimes she falls asleep, sometimes she just "rests." "A rest is as good as a sleep," she has said at least a hundred times. A thousand times?

Quietly I carry the *Metropolitan Toronto and Vicinity* telephone book from the hall into the kitchen and settle myself down at the table. I turn to the P's, running my finger down a column, looking for The Priory, Priory, the. For some reason my heart is beating wildly. But there is nothing listed. I look under the The's where I find quite a few listings: The Boutique, The Factory, The Place, The Shop, The Wiggery. But not The Priory. I even look under the B's for Brother Adam. There is no Brother Adam, (nor any other Brothers) then I try Adam, Brother. Nothing.

Perhaps the Priory is listed under Religious Houses or under Churches, but my mother has no Yellow Pages. I decide to phone Information.

It is necessary to whisper into the phone because my mother is resting a few yards away behind a closed door; she may even be sleeping. The operator is enraged by my muffled voice and my lack of specificity—"Did you say it was a church?"

"No."

"Well, is it or isn't it?"

"I'm not sure. I think it is but I'm not—"

"Is Adam the first name or last name?"

"His first. I think."

"I have to have a last name."

"I've got the address. It's on Beachview."

"Sorry. I need the last name."

"But I don't have it."

Actually, I reflect hanging up, it was absurd of me to think that a contemplative man like Brother Adam would have a telephone. Hadn't he implied in his many letters his ascetic obsession, his distrust of cramped, urban industrial society? A man like Brother Adam would never put himself in bondage to Bell Telephone; a man like Brother Adam would no sooner have a telephone than he would own a car. (He does, however, have a typewriter—all his letters were typewritten—but it is undoubtedly a manual model.)

I carry the phone book back to its place. I am not going to be able to phone Brother Adam after all. And it's too late now to drop him a note. I should have written from Vancouver as I had planned. What's the matter with me that I can't even make the simplest of social arrangements? I'll have to go to The Priory, there's no other solution. If I want to see him at all I will have to turn up at his door unannounced.

But I can't go today; my mother wouldn't like it if I disappeared on an unexplained errand, and besides Eugene is going to phone me from downtown at three o'clock. And tomorrow? Wednesday? Tomorrow is my day to

116

have lunch with Louis Berceau. Friday?—the wedding is on Friday, and Friday night we're flying back to Vancouver.

Thursday—if I go at all I'll have to go on Thursday. Yes, I will definitely go to see Brother Adam on Thursday. He is in the city, he is within a few miles of me, looking out of his window perhaps, sitting in the sun on his fire escape perhaps, and who knows, maybe he is writing a letter, perhaps even a letter to me, a letter beginning Dear Charleen, the sky is benignly blue today, the sun falls like a blessing across this page . . .

❧

Martin is restless. He has brought his chair inside; the sky has clouded over with alarming suddenness, and a few drops of heavy rain have already fallen onto the pages of his book. He is brooding mysteriously by the living room window.

I can never quite believe in the otherness of people's lives. That is, I cannot conceive of their functioning out of my sight. A psychologist friend once told me this attitude was symptomatic of a raging ego, but perhaps it is only a perceptual failure. My mother: every day she lives in this house; it is not all magically whisked away when I leave; the walls and furniture persist and so do the hours which she somehow fills. When Seth was five and started school I came home the first day after taking him and grieved, not out of nostalgia for his infancy or anxiety for his future, but for the newly revealed fact that he had entered into that otherness, that unseeable space which he must occupy forever and where not even my imagination could follow. It is the same with Martin who, year after unseen year, pursues objectives, lives through unaccountable weeks and months. Martin by the window, shut up in his thoughts, might be standing on the tip of the moon.

When my mother wakes up she goes into the kitchen

117

and begins browning a small pot roast on the back of the stove. "Nothing fancy," she explains. "I'm not going to fuss even for company, not at today's prices, not that there's anything wrong with a good honest pot roast and they don't give those away nowadays. Maybe it takes a few hours, you have to brown it really well, each side and the ends too, most people don't want to bother, they'd just as soon take a steak out of the freezer, never mind the cost, and call that a meal."

Because I make my mother nervous in the kitchen I go into the living room and stand beside Martin. He glances at his watch and says, "They should be home soon."

Is it a question or a statement? "You mean Judith?" I ask.

He nods.

"It's quite a distance," I remind him. "Remember? Out in the country somewhere."

"He's over seventy," Martin says grimly.

"Seventy-two," I nod.

"These old coots really shouldn't be on the road," Martin says with surprising ferocity.

The word "coots" shocks me; it seems a remarkably uncivilized word for Martin to use. What is the matter with him?

I spring to Louis's defence. "He seems alert enough for a man of his age. I'm sure he wouldn't drive if he felt he wasn't capable."

Martin looks again at his watch, and I can see by the involuntary snap of his wrist that he's seriously worried.

"I'm sure he's a careful driver," I insist again.

"But how do you *know*?"

I shrug. "He certainly didn't strike me as the reckless type."

"Didn't strike you," he says sourly, mockingly. But

118

then he asks seriously, "How *did* he strike you, Charleen?"

"Why are you so worried, Martin?"

"Because," Martin says, "have you considered that we don't know a damn thing about this man? Absolutely nothing."

"He used to be a Catholic," I say, as though that fact were exceptionally revealing, "and he used to teach carpentry or something like that. In a junior high. In the east end I think."

"Yes, yes," Martin says wearily, "but what do we *really* know about him?"

"His health, you mean?"

He sighs, faintly exasperated. "No, not his health. What I mean is, we don't know anything. Christ, maybe he's queer. Or maybe he molests children. Or sets fire to buildings or passes bum cheques. How would we know?"

I feel my mouth pulling into the shape of protest.

Martin continues, "He's an odd enough looking bird, you can see that. For your mother's sake we should have looked into him a bit more. And now here he goes off with Judith to God only knows where. We never even asked exactly where they were headed. And now a storm's coming up." He sighs again. "I don't know."

How odd Martin is becoming. I point out to him the obvious facts: that it is not even quite three o'clock yet, that it was after eleven when Judith and Louis left the house; that Louis distinctly said it was an hour's drive. True, we know next to nothing about him, but we couldn't very well call in a detective three days before the wedding; we would have to go by instinct, and my instinct—but would Martin believe it?—my instinct is to trust him. An odd-looking man, yes, and a strange marriage, perhaps—I nod in the direction of the kitchen—

but I feel certain, a certainty which I can in no way justify, that there is nothing to be afraid of.

Martin shakes his head, not entirely convinced but obviously wishing to be. He regards the empty street and the pulsing sky; the rain is holding back, squeezing laboured tears out of the scrambled grey clouds. Clearly Martin will not be happy until Judith is safely home; his devotion touches me, especially when I think of Judith's careless departure, how she went off without a thought about how Martin would pass the day, making a swift grab for her bag, yanking a cardigan over her shoulders; she took Louis's arm with huge, loping cheerfulness and sailed past the lilac tree; she drove away in his little Fiat without so much as a good-bye wave. And what else? Oh, yes, she hadn't told me about Martin's promotion; she hadn't, in fact, mentioned Martin at all; it is rather as though he were no more than a distant acquaintance.

I want to reassure Martin about Louis's reliability. "I don't know how to explain it," I tell him, "but I know Louis's okay. And I'm usually right about things like this." (Am I?)

He smiles a twisted, academic smile. "Intuition, I suppose."

I smile back. We will be friends. "Look," I say, "it's a rather odd marriage, but they may surprise us by being happy."

"Happy?" He looks amused at the idea.

"Well, a kind of happiness."

Happiness. Such a word, such a crude balloon of a word, such a flapping, stretched, unsightly female bladder of a word, how worn, how slack, how almost empty.

"Happiness," Martin repeats dully.

And before I can say anything more, the telephone rings. It's Eugene.

"Charleen."

"Yes. Eugene? How's it going? The conference?"

"Not bad. A bit draggy." (I rejoice at his detachment. If he had greeted me with ecstasy my heart would have sickened; I am queasy about misplaced enthusiasm.)

"What time are you coming?" I ask him.

"That's why I'm phoning. What I'd really like is if you could come downtown."

"Tonight?"

"We could have dinner." His voice slants with pleading. "Just the two of us."

"I don't know, Eugene. My mother. She's already making dinner. I don't know what she'd say."

"Couldn't you say I had to stay downtown later than I'd thought? Because of the conference?"

"I don't know, Eugene," I say doubtfully, thinking, poor Eugene, this morning must have been too much for him, and last night too, stuck in the back bedroom. Then I think of the pot roast my mother is cooking, reflecting that it is really rather small to feed all of us; wouldn't it, in fact, be a kindness to go out for dinner?

"Okay, Eugene. What time?"

"Any time. We're through for the day."

"I don't think I can make it before five," I tell him.

"Five then. Get a taxi and I'll wait for you at Bloor and Avenue Road."

"I'll come by subway. No need to take a taxi all the way from here."

"Charleen. Please."

"Eugene. I can't," I hiss into the phone. "My mother."

"It'll take you hours."

"No, it won't. Remember, I used to live here. I know the subway."

"You're crazy, you know. I'll be waiting. Bloor and Avenue Road, all right? By the museum."

"Okay," I promise. I think of my mother fretfully turning her pot roast in the kitchen, of Martin sighing by the window; suddenly I can't wait to get out of this house. "See you soon," I tell Eugene.

Of course my mother minds. Or, perhaps more accurately, she goes through the motions of minding; the pot roast has shrunk alarmingly.

"You might have said something about it this morning," she says with a short, injured sniff. "I could have done chops if I'd known there would be only three of us. I'm surprised your Dr. Redding, him a doctor and all, didn't have the courtesy to tell me this morning. It isn't like this was a hotel, whatever you may think. But go ahead, go ahead if you've made up your mind. All I say is it's a waste of money eating in fancy restaurants and you never know what you're getting, food poisoning, germs and I don't know what. I'd just as soon have a good honest pot roast if you asked me, not all that foreign food. You don't know what it is. I wouldn't have gone to the trouble of a pot roast if I thought you were going to take it into your head to go eat in a restaurant. I suppose you won't be too late?"

I listen; I bear with it; in a few minutes, I tell myself, she will have exhausted herself and I will be free to go. No, I tell her, we won't be too late. I speak calmly, lightly, remembering to be kind, reminding myself that her nerves are poor, that her health is shaky, that she has never, no never, eaten in a downtown restaurant, that she has been little rewarded in her life for her efforts: her scrambled eggs and careful housekeeping have not won her the regard she might have liked. I remind myself, above all, that she is weak.

And from her weakness flows not gentleness but a tidal wave of judgment. No wonder she has no friends. Over the years those few people who have approached her in friendship have been swept aside as prying and nosey, their gestures of help construed as malicious arrogance. Underpinning all her beliefs is the idea that people "should keep to themselves." They should stand on their own feet, they should mind their own business, they should look after their own, they should steer their own ship, they should tend their own gardens. Judgment colours her every encounter: "Mrs. Mallory said she admired my new slipcovers. Imagine that, she *admired* them. She couldn't just say she *liked* them, no, she *admired* them. I don't know what gives her the right to be so high and mighty. I've seen *her* slipcovers."

The world which she has constructed for herself is fiercely, cruelly, minutely competitive, a world in which each minimal victory requires careful registration. "Well," she would say, "I had my washing out first again today; first in the neighbourhood." Or, "At least we don't eat our dinner at five o'clock like the Hannas, only country people eat at five o'clock. I told Mrs. Hanna how we always sat down at six o'clock when my husband got home from the office, from the office I said, and that ended that."

My poor, self-tormented mother with her meaningless rage, her hollow vindictiveness, her shrinking fear—how had it happened? Heredity suggested a partial answer. My mother's mother, Elsie Gordon, had been one of two sisters born in a village in the Scottish lowlands; she had married a farmer named Angus Dunn, and the two of them had immigrated to Ontario where they rented and finally bought a thirty-acre farm and produced two daughters, Liddy (poor witless Aunt Liddy) and, three years later, Florence, our mother. And Florence, as though responding to a cry for symmetry, had also produced two daughters, Judith and me. So here we are, three generations of paired sisters; had we been shaped by a tradition of kindness and had our sensibility been monitored by learning, we might even have resembled Jane Austen's loving, clinging, nuance-addicted chains of sisters with their epistles and their fainting spells and their nervous agitation and their endless, garrulous, wonderful concern for one another. As it was, we were stamped out of rougher materials: dullness and drudgery, ignorance and self-preservation. Our father too had been a man without ancestors: to go back three generations was to find nothing but darkness; as the "Pome People" might say, our family tree was no more than a blackened stump. I don't even know the name of the Scottish village my grandparents came from. There have been no pilgrimages, there are no family legends, no family Bible with records of births and deaths, no brown-edged letters, no pressed flowers, few photographs and even those few stiffly obligatory; there are no family heirlooms and, of course, no family pride. Each generation has, it seems, effectively sealed itself off from its lowly forebears. My mother had not wanted to remember the muddy thirty acres where she grew up, the roofless barn, the doorless outhouse, the greasy kitchen table where the family took meals, the chickens which wandered in and out the back door, the thick-ankled mother who could neither read nor write and who had little capacity for affection or cleanliness. Hadn't my mother, in spite of all this, finished grade nine and hadn't she gone to Toronto to work in a hat factory? (Ah, but that was another sealed-off area.) Hadn't she married a city boy, someone who worked in an office, and hadn't they, after a few years, bought a house of their own, paid for it too, a real house in Scarborough with a back yard and plumbing, hadn't she kept it spotless and proved to everyone that she was just as good as the next person, hadn't she shown them? Yes.

Yes, yes, I understand it; why can't I put that understanding into motion? Why am I running down the sidewalk like this? The rain is pouring in sheets off the sides of my borrowed umbrella. My feet in my only good shoes are soaked already.

I'm on my way downtown, running to the subway station. How unfair to blame my mother for the fact that I am taking the subway—I clutch my scratched vinyl purse and admit the truth—I am the one who lacks the largesse to phone a taxi. Meagreness. I am Florence McNinn's daughter, the genes are there, nothing I've done has scratched them out.

My ankles are wet and rimmed with mud. Oh, God, one more block and at least I'll be out of the rain.

As I run splashing along, a sort of song thrums in my crazy head: Seth, Seth, where are you? Oh, Watson, why did you leave me? Brother Adam, why can't you save me? Eugene, Eugene, Eugene.

❧

Actually I love the subway. Not its denatured surfaces, not its weatherless tunnels, but its mad, anonymous, hyperactive, scrambling and sorting: the doors sliding open in the station, the rush of people, their faces declaring serious and purposeful journeys they are undertaking. Then another stop—they push their way out and are instantly replaced with equally serious, equally intent others. Their namelessness pleases me, their contained and dignified singularity comforts me. And it amazes me to think of the intricate, possibly secret connections between them, perhaps even connections of love. I like to think that at the end of each of these rushed, wordless, singular journeys, there is someone waiting, someone who is loved. How extraordinary—of course there are all sorts of chemical explanations—but still, how extraordinary is the chancy cement of love; a special dispensation which no one ever really deserves but which almost everyone gets a little of. Even my unloving mother has found someone finally to love. Even Louis Berceau with his scraped-out lungs and his screwed-up, druid face has found someone to love.

Joy seizes me fiercely, sweetly. I am one of the lucky ones after all with my hard-as-a-kernel nut of indestructibility. My hereditary disease, the McNinn syndrome, has riddled me with cowardice, no question about it, but happiness will always return from time to time—as on this train blindly tunnelling beneath Bay and Bloor.

At the end of the trip, above ground, Eugene is waiting, his gull-grey raincoat flapping in the wind and his face fixed with its own peculiar flat uncertainty. I am ridiculously happy to see him.

Eugene steers me into a taxi and down the street toward a big, new hotel; through the chrome-framed doors into a warm, bronze-sheeted lobby, strenuously contemporary with revolving lucite chandeliers and motorized waterfalls. The elevator is a cube of perfect creature comfort: softly lit and carpeted, ventilated, soundless and swift.

In a darkened cocktail lounge high over the city, Eugene and I sit on strangely shaped, grotesquely padded chairs and sip long, cold drinks and nibble on tiny smoked, salty, crackling things. And we talk in the strange, curiously-shy fashion of reunited lovers. I tell Eugene about Louis Berceau, and he tells me about an old dental school friend he ran into today who asked him how "his charming wife was." When Eugene told him he was now divorced, the friend backed off and, in a blind flurry of honesty, said, "Actually I never could stand Jeri." Or was it honesty, Eugene wonders now, drumming his fingers on the table. Maybe the friend was, belatedly and pointlessly, scrambling for sides.

Maybe he was trying in an unfocussed way to comfort Eugene or to congratulate him for having rid himself of an unpleasant wife. "Strange," Eugene murmurs, looking into his gin and tonic. "Strange how people react to divorce. Not knowing whether sympathy is in order or not."

I agree with him. Death is so much simpler; the rituals are firmer, shapelier; social custom will never be able to alter or diminish the effect of death; one need never be confused about the proper response.

Later, in the restaurant, we eat marvellous little things from a wagon of hors d'oeuvres. Tiny fishes, oily and frilled with lemon; sculptured vegetables lapped with mayonnaise, glazed and healthy under parsley coverlets, sharp little sausages and miniature onions, gherkins and lovely, lovely olives, black, green, some of them an astonishing pink. After that we have tornedos in cream (the speciality of the house, the beaming, gleaming waiter tells us.) I eat less guiltily knowing Eugene will be able to write off almost every penny this meal is costing; at the same time I feel our feast is meanly diminished by that very fact. A paradox. Eugene says he feels the same way. Why?

He says it is a question of puritan ethic: you can only enjoy what you have laboriously worked for. Pleasure must be paid for by sacrifice, at least for those like us. It must not come too easily or too soon. He shakes his head sadly over the fact, but accepts it, admitting that most middle class rewards will no doubt continue to elude him.

"It might be better for the kids though," he says, speaking of his two boys, Sandy and Donny, who live with Jeri and stay with him in his apartment most weekends. He is always impressed with their unalloyed enjoyment of the presents he gives them. "They don't think they have to do a damn thing in return," he says. "I mean, God, they're little primitives. They just open their arms to whatever rains down on them. Damned ungrateful too, but maybe that's better than being screwed up with the debt-to-the-devil complex."

"Maybe," I say. And yet I'm glad Eugene is not entirely guilt-free about tax deductions; I'm grateful for his company here on the ethical edge, in the no-man's-land between youth and age, between puritan guilt and affluent hedonism; what a pair we are, half-educated, half-old, half-married, half-happy. I should marry him and relieve a little of the guilt he suffers. He would like that: living alone in an apartment is frightening for a man like Eugene; he feels his ordinariness more than ever. Maybe I will marry him. What a nice man he is. I don't even mind his being an orthodontist. What if his proportions are less than heroic? Isn't goodwill a kind of prehensile heroism in this century? Does it really matter that Doug Savage thinks he is miserably average, even slightly substandard, and that Greta fears his mediocrity will place a ruinous stain on Seth's character? I cannot, after all, choose a husband just to please my friends.

Nothing is simple. After dinner we take a taxi back to Scarborough, sitting in the back seat with our arms around each other. The sky has cleared; there's a rounded, whited, theatrical moon cleanly cruising along behind us. Eugene's raincoat is still damp and rather cold against my thighs but I like the feel of his lips on my face, unhurried, soft.

❧

Coming into my mother's dimly lit living room with its flickering television screen and its cleanly shabby furniture, my senses play a perceptual trick on me: I see, it seems, not those who are actually there—my mother with her mending, Judith with her book, and Martin with his newspaper—but the ghostly shadowed presence of those who are missing. My father—shy, secretive, stoic, perpetually embarrassed—reading his paper much as Martin does, with hunched concentration as though he were perched temporarily in a doctor's waiting room. And Judith's children, Richard and Meredith: their absence is marked by her weary inattentiveness to the novel she's reading, the way she jerks the pages over; her real life belongs to another place now. And Seth, the grandson my mother has not even inquired about, the grandson for whom she does not knit mittens or mufflers and whose birthdays she does not remember (he is, after all, the extension of a daughter who has twice disgraced her family, first by running away and then by getting divorced); Seth who is the most important person in my world is suddenly briefly visible, filling this little room with his absence.

"Seth!" I suddenly exclaim.

"What's the matter?" Judith says, looking up.

"I've forgotten to phone Seth."

"It's not too late, is it?" Eugene asks, hanging up his raincoat.

"Do you mean long distance?" my mother asks.

"I just want to see if he's all right."

"But it's long distance."

"It's after eleven," Judith says helpfully. "Don't the rates go down after eleven?"

"After twelve, I think," Martin says.

"It's all right," I tell my mother. "I'll leave the money for the call."

"A waste of money," she shrugs. "And when you've been out to a restaurant and everything."

"I really must see how he is."

"But you're going home Friday night. Why would you want to go and run up the phone bill for nothing?"

"But I have to. I really must," I insist, knowing I sound unreasonable and shrill. "I simply couldn't sleep a wink tonight unless I know everything is all right."

"But what could go wrong?" my mother says giving one last dying protest.

"There's the phone ringing *now*," Eugene says. "Maybe it's Seth calling *you*."

But it isn't Seth. It's Doug Savage and he's phoning from Calgary.

"Hiya, Char," he says as breezily as though he were phoning from next door.

"Doug!" I stumble, a little confused. "Well, hello."

There is a short pause—perhaps we have a poor connection—and then I hear Doug saying, "Just wanted to tell you not to worry."

"Worry?"

"Just wanted to let you know everything's fine."

"But . . . but what are you doing in Calgary?"

"Oh, you know me, just a little trip. Always here, there, or somewhere."

"And Greta?"

Another pause. "Has Greta phoned you at all?"

"No. Was she going to?"

He hesitates. "Just thought she might give you a buzz."

"Well, no she hasn't, but as a matter of fact I thought I'd phone her tonight. Have a word or two with Seth."

"Oh, God, Char, save your shekels. As a matter of fact, I don't think they're home tonight anyway."

"Are you sure?"

"Yes. Yes, I'm sure. Something about the band. A rehearsal, I think."

"Oh," I say, feeling suddenly let down and disappointed. "I forgot about that."

"Well, don't let it worry you. Everything's fine. Fine." His voice trails off.

"Maybe I'll try tomorrow night."

"Great idea. You do that. Having a good time?"

"What? Oh, yes, uhuh, a good time."

"Take care then. Bye for now."

"Bye, Doug. And Doug . . .?"

"Yeah?"

"Thanks for calling. That was really nice of you to think of phoning. But why . . . I mean why exactly *did* you phone me?"

"Didn't want you worrying, that's all. Just thought I'd let you know everything's fine. Good night then, baby."

"Good night," I say. And stupidly, cheerfully, add, "Sleep tight."

Chapter 5

"She never talks to me anymore," Judith is saying of her daughter Meredith. "Not the way she used to when she was a little girl."

Children. Judith and I lie in bed listening to our mother in the kitchen making breakfast and we talk about our children.

"I'm always reading those articles about how parents are supposed to keep the lines of communication open," Judith says. "And now and then out of duty I make a stab at it."

"And what happens?"

"Nothing. Absolutely nothing. She—Meredith—just smiles. Mona Lisa. At least *sometimes* she smiles. Other times she cringes. As though the thought that we might have something in common was unspeakable. Everyone's always telling me how charming she is, and it's true she's got this non-McNinn effervescence. And a kind of wild originality too, but to me she doesn't say one word."

"You don't sound as though you mind all that much," I say.

"Mind? Oh, I suppose I should. After all, I'm her mother, she's my only daughter, why shouldn't she be able to pour out her heart now and then. But the truth is, Charleen, I couldn't bear it if she did. All that anguish."

"You must be curious though."

"In a way. I'm always wondering what she's thinking

about. Or what she does when she's not home. After all, she's eighteen. But eighteen is such a . . . well . . . such a suffering age. Remember? Sometimes I feel I've only just recovered from it myself. To listen to her ups and downs would kill me, and I think she knows it too. She senses it. She's got a kind of rare psychic radar—she always had but now and then she looks so bedeviled that I'm afraid she's going to break down and take me into her confidence. She's come close a couple of times. But then she stops herself. I can almost see her mumbling her vows of silence. And, strangely enough, I'm rather proud of her for it, for going it alone. I admire her for it. And I'm grateful, even though I know I'm failing her somehow, I'm grateful to be left alone."

"What about Richard?" I ask her.

"Richard," she shrugs. "He's always kept things to himself. Of course he's a boy. They're always more secretive. I suppose that's what you call a sexist judgment. Does Seth confide in you?"

I pause for a moment, not really wanting to admit that he doesn't. "No," I say slowly, "but I don't think it means anything."

It's true that most of the time these days Seth and I speak to each other in monosyllables—sure, yeah, okay—but these words are our accepted coinage of familiarity, the sort of shorthand which forms unconsciously between people who are naturally in harmony. It has never occurred to me to think that his lack of explicit communication might be an attempt to hide something from me; his nature has always been exceedingly open, and, if anything, it is this openness that worries me, openness with a suggestion of vacuum, a curious, perhaps dangerous acquiescence.

"I used to think it was strange," Judith is saying, "that we never told Mother anything when we were girls. All my friends used to rush home and tell their mothers everything. But we never did. At least I never did."

"Neither did I," I say firmly. "Never once."

"You know," Judith says thoughtfully, "looking back, I don't think it's all that strange. I think she must have sent out a kind of warning signal, a thought wave, saying 'Don't tell me anything because I've got enough to cope with as it is.'"

"Perhaps," I nod.

"Anyway," Judith continues, "I've come to the place now where I know she and I will never be able to talk. I'm absolutely sure of it."

Her certainty surprises me; it seems rather shocking to be so final, and I am forced to admit to myself that I have by no means surrendered. Somehow—it is only a question of finding the point of entry—I will break through our terrible familial silence. I came close, very close, yesterday drying the eggbeater.

Judith springs out of bed and begins to get dressed, but I lie under the blanket a few minutes longer; I am still sleepy, my mind begins to wander, but I am not thinking about Meredith or Judith or about my mother or even about the girl I once was. For some reason I am thinking about Seth. And the small string of worry that plucks away at me.

❧

After breakfast—toast and coffee in the kitchen—we take up yesterday's small routines. Eugene goes downtown for his conference, and Martin carries his newspaper into the back yard. It is rather cool outside; a wooly sun struggling through massed clouds, the grass still wet from yesterday's rain. My mother sets up the ironing board in the kitchen (the smell and sight of its scorched cover pierces me with nostalgia) and she presses, through a clean, damp tea towel, the dress she will wear for her wedding. Cocoa-brown crimpeline with raised ribs, a row of dull, wood-looking buttons down the front, long sleeves and no collar.

"It came with a scarf," she says, frowning narrowly, "as if a scarf made up for no collar." Her lips turn inward thinly, visible, measurable emblem of her complaint. "But I'm certainly not going to wear it, all those bright colours, cheap, of course it was in the March sales; nothing is well made anymore, imagine not even a collar. But it will have to do, that's all there is to it."

I am thinking: the wedding is Friday, tomorrow is Thursday and with luck I'll be seeing Brother Adam at last. Today is Wednesday; today I am having lunch with Louis. He is coming for me at eleven. When I asked Judith if she enjoyed her lunch yesterday, she smiled somewhat mysteriously. "It was interesting," she said.

"Did you find out anything about Louis?" I asked.

"A little," she smiled, "and so will you."

For a moment I pondered this, and then I asked, "Where did you go?"

"A little place in the country."

"Where exactly?" I pressed her.

"West of Toronto. Weedham. Just a little spot."

"Weedham? Weedham, Ontario? Are you sure?"

"Yes," she had answered, puzzled. "Weedham. Spelled WEEDHAM. Being literal-minded, I naturally expected it to be full of weeds but it turned out to be a pretty little place. You'll like it."

Weedham. Weedham, Ontario. Watson. I am going to Weedham, Ontario. I am going there today. An arc of anticipation, not unlike sexual desire, brightens inside me. I look at the kitchen clock. Nine-thirty. In an hour and a half I will be sitting in Louis Berceau's little green Fiat bouncing along the road to Weedham, Ontario.

❧

I am sick, oh, I am sick with shame, I am in hell. I

135

want to die of it, oh God, such pain, such humiliation, to be so humiliated. Stupid, stupid, I am sick with shame, it won't go away, it's done, nothing will take it away, dear God.

I am lying on my mother's bed in the middle of the morning, I am rocking from side to side, my fists in my eyes. I want to moan out loud, I want to weep, but no one must hear me, no one must know, oh, the shame of it.

Martin. Martin knows. Will he tell Judith? I cannot bear the thought of Judith knowing. She would think it was—what?—she would think it was *amusing,* too amusing for words. It would be awful to hear her laughing over it; I couldn't stand that.

Yet, isn't it her fault, isn't she the cause of it's happening? If I hadn't been thinking about her and her peculiar baffling indifference to Martin, it would never have happened.

She had been so busily occupied after breakfast. She had settled down at the dining room table with her portable typewriter and her reference books and her lovely calf-hide attaché case which she snapped open on her lap; inside were bundles of five-by-seven cards, each bundle bound with a rubber band; I thought of the way Mafia men carry their wads of money. Her notes, she explained, and with an air of enormous concentration she had selected one bundle, had whipped off the rubber band with a clean snap, and, one by one, she arranged the cards around her in a large semi-circle, a zombie playing at solitaire. I watched admiringly, such concentration, such independence. Judith explained that she had set herself a deadline for her next book. "It's odd," she said to me, "I seem to be getting compulsive in my old age. Writing used to be just a kind of hobby. Now if a single day goes by without working, I feel as though the day's been lost."

Martin, on his way in from the back yard to get his book, had paused and regarded her affectionately. Judith gave him a level look over her circle of cards; she looked at him, but I could tell she didn't really see him; what she gave him was a wide spatial stare, an empty optic greeting as though he were a smallish portion of the wallpaper; then she broke her gaze abruptly, scratched her head with vigour and, slowly, thoughtfully, inserted a sheet of paper into her typewriter.

Martin picked up his book and went outside, and out of a kind of pity—I think that's what it was—I followed him.

For a few minutes we sat together on the back steps, letting the frail, glassy sunlight fall on our backs. The little lawn looked exceptionally fine. Louis had put some fertilizer on it, my mother had explained with her mixture of shyness and sarcasm, and two pounds of grass seed. Martin seemed rather lonely, rather bored, a little restless, he seemed glad enough of my company. I even dared to tease him a little about how he'd worried about Judith's outing with Louis; he had laughed at himself in an altogether pleasant way, and then we talked for a few minutes about modern criticism. Yes, we were starting to be friends. We were comfortable sitting there together; the sun was growing stronger; it might be a nice day after all, and I was just about to say so when Martin leaned over and whispered into my ear.

"Look, Charleen, just between us, what do you think of the archaic sleeping arrangements here?"

"Pardon?" I said. Our mother had always taught us to say pardon.

"The sleeping arrangements," he repeated. "You know, the boys' dorm and the girls' dorm."

"Well—" I started to say.

He leaned closer, he put his arm around my shoulder,

he whispered in my ear, "How about switching around tonight?"

"Martin!" I breathed, completely shaken.

"We could switch back later," he leered. "No one would ever know."

"Martin," I said again in a dazed whisper, "I couldn't. I couldn't possibly."

There was a short chilly silence. A dead hole of a silence.

Then Martin asked, "Why not?"

I stood up abruptly, choking back rage, "Because Judith happens to be my sister. My own sister. What kind of person do you think I am?"

"My good Christ, Charleen, don't go all moral on me."

"And what makes you think I would want to sleep with you anyway?"

Then, then Martin's expression underwent a profound shocking, nightmarish change. Then suddenly he began to laugh, very softly so that my mother, still ironing in the kitchen, wouldn't hear. Manic tears squeezed out of the corners of his eyes, he rocked back and forth on the step hugging himself, "Oh, Charleen, oh, my God, I can't stand it, it's so funny. I didn't mean you and me. Oh, God." He broke into another obscene spasm of laughter.

I stared. What was he laughing about? Had he gone crazy?

Then quite suddenly I understood. Then I knew.

"I meant you and Eugene," Martin gasped. "And Judith and me. After all," he continued, making an effort at control, "we are joined in holy wedlock and all that."

I hardly heard him. I dashed away, up the steps and through the back door. I ran past my mother and here I am in the bedroom, rocking and moaning in a suffering parody of Martin rocking and moaning on the back steps. How he laughed. I could die, I could die, I wish I could die.

*

Louis will be here any minute. I roll over in bed and look at the clock. I must get changed. I must try to look cheerful and eager and grateful to be taken on an outing.

I put on my stockings and slip into my new orange dress. Then I brush my hair, trying to turn it under smoothly the way Mr. Mario had done. It doesn't look too bad. And the dress looks surprisingly becoming. I even hum to myself a jerky little comforting tune while I clean my shoes with a Kleenex. They're still a little damp from yesterday.

Too bad about Martin, I say to myself in mock dismissal, peering into the mirror. Just when we were starting to be friends. If only I'd laughed I might have carried it off. Ah well, with my typical faulty reflex I blow it every time, a fatal quarter-step behind the rest of the world. Martin, without a doubt, will have been repelled by my embarrassment; not only that, but I with my gross misinterpretation have left myself vulnerable to a host of other questions: exactly what kind of a woman was I anyway? Just answer that.

Then I hear the little car pulling up in front, I hear Louis and Martin in the back yard talking about lawn care. One last reassuring grimace in the mirror and I emerge.

Louis does not embrace me, but he gives me a smile and a cherishing handshake over the kitchen table. My mother, sighing as she puts away the ironing board, says sharply, "Don't be too late. I'm making my tunafish bake for supper."

We walk to the car; Louis is cheerful and nimble and I shorten my steps to match his. The sun is blazing merrily overhead, and Martin and Judith walk with us to the street; Judith's writing is going well this morning and she seems immoderately happy. "Have a good afternoon," she sings.

I don't dare look at Martin. But after Louis has turned the ignition and we start to slide away from the curb, I turn back and find my eyes looking directly into his. His eyes look funny as though he is squinting into the sun. No, he isn't, no he isn't. He is—yes—he is winking at me.

Without thinking, without reflecting, I wink back, and then we move down the street, Louis and I, slowly, almost elegantly.

❧

Louis's car is a Fiat 600, a 1968 model, recently repainted, the interior worn but exceedingly clean. This is the car that takes my mother back and forth to the cancer clinic, this is the car that carries her out for Sunday drives, this is the car which in two days will become their car, used for their minor errands, for their weekly trips to the Dominion Store, for their little jaunts into the country.

Louis, as I had predicted, is a cautious driver. He sits tightly in the driver's seat, moving the steering wheel and gearshift with intense little jerks, with careful, choppy, concentrated deliberation. The car moves down the suburban streets, delicately shuddering, and Louis, leaning forward, appears rather gnomelike with his wreaths of wrinkles, his puckered, colourless mouth, his contained and benign ugliness. Taking the 401 he heads west across the city.

On the way to Weedham Louis talks about the wedding. And I think how strange that it is so easy for people to talk in cars. It must have something to do with the enforced temporary proximity or with the proportion of

140

space or perhaps the sealed, cushioned interior silence which must resemble, in some way, the insulated room where Greta Savage meets each week with her encounter group. It is as though the automobile were a specially designed glass talking-machine engineered for human intimacy. Furthermore, in a car the need to watch the road diverts and relieves the passengers, giving to their conversation an unexpected flowing disinterestedness.

Louis clears his throat and explains that both he and my mother were anxious to avoid fuss and expense; that was why they decided to be married in my mother's living room in the middle of the afternoon. Afterwards there would be tea in the dining room. And a small cake which Louis has ordered from a bakery; a United Church minister, a local man, has been asked to perform the ceremony.

This last piece of information surprises me. The McNinns have always been vaguely Protestant; at least Protestant is the word Judith and I supplied when we were asked our religious denomination. But we had never been a church-going family. The reason: I am not entirely sure, but it stemmed, I think, from my mother's belief that people only go to church in order to show off their hats and fur coats and to sneer at those less elegantly dressed. Certainly it had nothing to do with those larger issues such as the existence of God or the requirement of worship.

"Is anyone else going to be at the wedding?" I ask Louis. No, he answers, only the family. He himself has no family, none at all anymore.

The neighbours. I wonder if the neighbours have any inkling that my mother is to be remarried on Friday. Has she told anyone or has she kept her secret? The leitmotif of her anxiety, for as long as I can remember, has been her fear of being judged by the neighbours; what would the neighbours think? When twenty years ago I ran away with Watson to Vancouver, she had been struck almost incoherent with shame: what would the neighbours think? All the other girls in the neighbourhood were going on to secretarial school or studying to be hairdressers, but her daughter—the shame of it—had eloped with a student, had left a note on her pillow and ridden off to Vancouver on the back of a motorcycle.

Later I learned from Judith exactly how shattered she had been, how for months she'd hardly left the house, how for years she'd been unable to look the neighbours in the face. The fact that I had not been pregnant as she had supposed, the fact that Watson and I had been quite legally if rather sloppily married before we set off for the west, and the fact that Watson, three years later, received his Ph.D. (with honours)—none of these things seemed to ease the terrible shame of my extraordinary departure. And then the divorce, the embarrassing blow of the divorce which for years I tried to conceal from her. No one else in the neighbourhood had a daughter who was divorced. The neighbours had daughters who were buying property in Don Mills and producing families of children who came visiting on Sundays. Our mother alone had been cursed by strange daughters: Judith with her boisterous disturbing honesty, bookish and careless, and I with my now fatherless child, my unprecedented divorce, my books of poetry. The neighbours' children hadn't dismayed and defeated and failed their mothers.

And now my mother is getting married and she doesn't, it seems, worry at all about what the neighbours will think. She doesn't care a fig; she doesn't care a straw. For after all these years she has, in a sense, triumphed over the neighbours. Or, more accurately, the neighbours no longer exist. Both Mr. and Mrs. Maddison with their wailing cats and shredded curtains have died. The MacArthurs—lazy Mrs. MacArthur, always hanging out the clothes in her dressing gown, and Mr. MacArthur with his gravel truck sitting by the side of the house—have moved to a duplex in Riverdale to be near their married daughter. The Whiteheads—he drank, she used filthy language—have gone to California. Mrs. Lilly and her crippled sister, so sinfully proud of their dahlias, have disappeared without a trace, and the Jacksons, whom my mother believed to be very common, have become rich and live in south Rosedale. All the houses in our neighbourhood are filled with Jamaicans now, with Pakistanis, with multi-generation, unidentifiable southern Europeans who grow cabbages and kohlrabi in their backyards and rent out their basements. My mother is not in the least afraid of their judgment on her. She has, after all, lived for forty years in her little house, she has lived on the block longer than anyone else, she is widowed old Mrs. McNinn, the woman who keeps a clean house, the woman who minds her own business; she is respectable old Mrs. McNinn.

❧

"We're almost there," Louis says, steering carefully. "Another mile or so."

"What a pretty little town," I exclaim. For Weedham, Ontario, in the blond, spring sunlight has a tidy green rural face. A sign announces its population: 2,500. Another sign welcomes visiting Rotarians. Still another, a billboard of restrained proportions, urges visitors to stop at the Wayfarers' Inn.

"That's where we're going," Louis says.

The Wayfarers' Inn at the edge of town is relatively new, built in the last thirty years or so, but in the style of more ancient inns it has a stone courtyard, a raftered ceiling, here and there curls of wrought iron, and rows of polished wooden tables ranged round the walls. Light filters glowingly through stained glass windows which, Louis explains, are the real thing; they were taken from an old house in the area which was being demolished.

"It's charming," I say politely.

Shyly he tells me, "I brought your mother here for lunch. When I asked her to marry me."

I am taken by surprise. In fact, I am dumbfounded, for I cannot imagine my mother submitting to the luxury of lunch at the Wayfarers' Inn. And it is even more difficult to imagine her absorbing—in this room at one of these little tables peopled with local businessmen and white-gloved club women—a declaration of love.

"Was it . . . sudden?" I dare to ask.

His face crinkles over his mushroom soup, engulfed in pleasant nostalgia. "Yes," he nods, choking a little. "Only three months after we'd met at the clinic."

His openness touches me, but at the same time I am unbelievably embarrassed. Much as I would like to pursue it, to ask him, "and do you really love each other?" I cannot; Judith might have, in fact she probably did. I am certain he told her too, just as I am certain he would tell me if I asked; why else has he brought me out for lunch if not to make me feel easy about him. But I draw back, I can't ask, not now at least. To pursue the subject beyond Louis's first eager revelation might diminish it, might bury it. Why shouldn't he love my mother? If there *is* such a thing as justice, then surely even the unloving deserve love. She's like everyone else, I suddenly see; inside her head are the same turning, gathering spindles of necessity; why shouldn't he love her?

Louis smiles at me with almost boyish gaiety, his teeth, dark ivory with flashes of gold at the sides, his wrinkles breaking like waves around the hub of his happiness—a happiness so accidental, so improbable and so finely suspended—hadn't Brother Adam written that happiness arrives when least expected and that it tends to dissolve under scrutiny. Better to change the subject.

I glance around the room, taking in the polished wood and coloured glass; a square of ruby-red light falls on Louis's soft old hair. "How did you find this place?" I ask him. "Had you been here before . . . before the day . . . you brought her out here?"

"Oh, yes, yes, yes," he is pleased with my question. "When I was teaching school—I used to be the wood-work teacher, your mother must have told you. Always was good with my hands." He spreads them for my inspection.

"Simple carpentry, nothing complicated, knife racks and wall shelves mostly. At the end of the school year, round about the middle of June, I'd say, we used to come out here, all the teachers, and have lunch." He coughs, a sudden attacking hack of a cough. "Sort of, you know, a celebration."

"Which school was it?" I ask politely.

"St. Vincent." He chokes again. "Not so far from where you went to school."

"St. Vincent," I say, remembering. "That's a Catholic school, isn't it?"

He nods, watching me closely.

"Some of the kids in our neighbourhood used to go there," I tell Louis. "The MacArthurs. Billy MacArthur? Red hair, fat, always in trouble?"

"I don't think I remember him," Louis says regretfully.

"Judith and I always kind of envied the Catholic kids. It seemed—I don't know—sort of exotic going to a school like that. Like a pageant. First communion and all those white dresses. And veils even. And catechism. And always calling their teachers Sister this and Father that."

Louis nods and smiles.

"But," I say thoughtfully, "I always thought that the teachers in those days had to be nuns and priests."

Louis nods again.

"But you . . ."

"Yes," Louis says.

Silence. "A priest?" I whisper.

"Yes," he says in a level voice, "a priest."

"I can't believe it."

"I wanted you to know."

"Does Judith . . ."

"I told her yesterday."

"And my mother. Of course she . . ."

"Of course."

"But—" I try to gather in my words, I struggle for the right words but there don't seem to be any for this moment, "but weren't you . . . I thought . . . weren't you married before?"

"Only to the Church," he says with a faint, modest rhetorical edge.

"But now . . ."

"I made the decision to leave," he says, "three years ago."

My mother is marrying a sick, seventy-two-year-old ex-priest, I can hardly breath, I cannot believe this.

"But Louis," I stumble on, "why did you . . . I mean, it's none of my business . . . but why did you leave?"

He is ready to tell me; he has, I can see, brought me here to make me understand. "It was when I first started to . . . get sick. I know it seems strange. You'd think sickness would make me cling to my vocation. But it wasn't like that."

"What was it like then?"

"I started to feel afraid."

"Of death?"

"I could never be frightened of death. I'm still a Catholic."

"What were you afraid of then?" I ask, but already I know. Oh, Louis, I know what it is to be afraid.

"I wasn't sure. I'm still not sure now. But I think I was afraid I'd missed half my life."

For a sickening half-instant I think he is referring to celibacy, surely he doesn't mean that.

"I'd never lived alone," Louis explains carefully. "I'd never had the strength. But then, when I got sick, it seemed possible. Anything seemed possible. It doesn't make sense, I know."

But to me it does make sense, for why had I married Watson? Because his sudden arrival into my life had said one thing: anything was possible. Possibility rimmed those first days like a purplish light; love was possible; flight was possible; my whole life was going to be possible.

"So you decided to leave?" I say to Louis.

He nods. His face has become alarmingly flushed. How difficult this must be for him. I want to reach out and pat his arm, but I'm too awestruck to move.

"I've been quite happy," he says, "surprisingly so. Of course, being alone has its problems too."

I know. I know.

"Then I met your mother."

I smile uncertainly.

He makes a little laced basket of his hands and says, "I hope you don't think . . . you don't think we're just old and foolish."

"Of course not," I gasp truthfully.

"Because we don't have . . ." he pauses, "surely you

realize . . . we don't have all that . . . much time." He says this lightly, he even gives a faint, ghoulish, baffling sort of chuckle which I find both shocking and admirable.

Now I *do* reach out and pat his hand, his chamois-coloured, brown-spotted, hairless little hand. We sit in the red and yellow and blue pooled light without saying a word. A young waitress takes our plates away and brings us ice cream in tiny imitation pewter bowls.

Louis sighs at last and says thickly, "It would have been nice . . . nice . . . to have a priest at the wedding, that's all. It doesn't matter though. Not really."

"You mean to perform the ceremony?" I ask him.

"Oh no. That would be a little . . . uncomfortable for your mother, I think. But it would have been nice to have a priest, just to, you know, be there."

"Couldn't you invite one?" I ask him earnestly.

"It's awkward," he says. "I'm a little . . . out of touch."

I tease the bitter chocolate ice cream with the tip of my spoon. I can't stop myself: I say, "Look, Louis, I know a priest. As a matter of fact I'm going to see him tomorrow. Why don't I ask him to come? I don't have to tell him anything about your being a priest. I could just invite him—you know—to my mother's wedding."

He tips his head to one side and smiles a startled amber-toothed asymmetrical smile; pleasure drains into his grouted eyes and, nodding his head, he surprises me by saying, "Why, that would be very kind of you."

❧

Louis's confession has refreshed him; he looks rather tired but he orders coffee with the happy air of a man who has discharged his purpose.

For me the revelation is not so speedily digested; it hangs overhead like a bank of fresh steam, and my imagination struggles to picture Louis of the clerical collar;

Louis of the ivory Sunday vestments, wafer in mouth, cup upraised; Louis as devout young novice; Louis as frightened lonely child—somewhere under the old, soft, yellowed skin that boy must still exist. It is too much for me—the idea of Louis as priest resists belief, but it must, it will be, assimilated.

And what, I ask myself, is so strange about my mother meeting a defrocked priest—an ex-priest, I should say, it is somehow kinder to think of him that way—certainly a lot of them are floating around these days. And how did I imagine they would look if not like Louis? Did I expect them to be exhausted and spiritual, hollow-eyed, pitted with recognizable piety, baroque in manner, fatherly and frightened with damaged holiness sewn into their fingertips? They were men, only men, assorted, various and unmarked. Was Eugene with his moist normalcy and gentle hands identifiable as an orthodontist? And Martin: to see him turning over the pages of the *Globe and Mail* in my mother's back yard, who would suspect the Miltonic peaks and canyons that furnished his intelligence: the very idea was ridiculous.

Meeting Watson Forrest when I was eighteen—there he was drinking orange soda in a run-down, soon-to-be-bankrupt drugstore—a short, frowsy boy of twenty-two with wrinkled corduroy pants, acne scars and tufted crown of reddish hair—I had not believed him at first when he told me he had graduated in botany from the University of Toronto, that he had already written his Master's thesis (what was a Master's thesis? I had asked) on rare Ontario orchids. Later, made restless by the romance of the North, Watson had turned to Arctic lichens; later still, drawn into the back-to-nature movement, he had focussed on the common pigweed and had theorized, often tiresomely, on the pigweed's ability to draw nutrients to the surface of the earth. Orchids to pigweed: Watson had continually evolved toward the more popular, more democratic, more ubiquitous forms of a plant life. Specialty was for those who were content to stand still. Watson had resisted, more than most, the stamp of profession.

And as for me, Charleen Forrest, who, seeing me buying oranges in the Safeway or mailing letters on rainy Vancouver corners, who would guess that I am a poet? My bone structure is wrong; all those elongations; all those undisciplined edges, the ridged thighs, the wire-brush hair, the corns on my feet, the impurities in my heart—how could I possibly be a poet, how could I, as some might say, sing in a finer key?

The truth is, I am a sort of phony poet; poetry was grafted artificially onto my lazy unconnectedness, and it was Watson—yes, Watson—who did the grafting. Watson made me a poet—at least he pushed me in that direction—by his frenzied, almost hysterical efforts to educate me. What a shock it must have been, when he recovered from the first sexual ecstasies, to find himself married to an eighteen-year-old girl of crushing ignorance. Our first apartment in Vancouver was crammed with the books he brought me from the library, books I read doggedly, despairingly, in an attempt to conceal from him the shallowness of my learning. I seemed always to be working against time; the bright lights of possibility he had lighted in my head were already flickering out one by one.

I took a short typing course in Vancouver and for three years I supported both of us by typing term papers for graduate students in the cluttered, dusty nest of our one-room apartment. And in between, in order to forestall Watson's ultimate disenchantment, I sweated through books of history, biography, science; in fact, whatever Watson selected for me. How he had loved the role of tutor, one of his many incarnations: he became a kind of magician and I the raw material to be transformed. His devotion to my education was, to be sure, less than altruistic: his first appointment was in sight; another incarnation, another role—that of brilliant young lecturer—awaited him, and he became, not without reason, worried about the handicap of a stupid wife.

Somewhere along the line my self-education ceased to be a wifely duty. Watson began edging into student politics and laying the groundwork for the *Journal*, and for me, sitting alone in the apartment, literature became a friend and ally. Surrounded by frayed basket chairs, brick-and-board book shelves, a card table desk, studio couch and bamboo blinds—the furniture, in fact, of the newly married—literature became the real world. And poetry, modern poetry, unlocked in me not so much a talent, but a strange narrow aptitude, a knack, at first, and nothing more.

My first poems were experiments; I built them on borrowed rhythms; I was a dedicated tinkerer, putting together the shapes and ideas which I shoplifted. And images. Like people who excel at crossword puzzles, I found that I could, with a little jiggling, produce images of quite startling vividness. My first poems (pomes) were lit with a whistling blue clarity (emptiness) and they were accepted by the first magazine I sent them to. Only I knew what paste-up jobs they were, only I silently acknowledged my debt to a good thesaurus, a stimulating dictionary and a daily injection, administered like Vitamin B, of early Eliot. I, who manufactured the giddy dark-edged metaphors, knew the facile secret of their creation. Like piecework I rolled them off. Never, never, never did I soar on the wings of inspiration; the lines I wrote, hunched over the card table in that grubby, poorly ventilated apartment, were painstakingly assembled, an artificial montage of poetic parts. I was a literary con-man, a quack, and the size of my early success was amazing, thrilling and frightening.

But after Watson left us, after he walked out on Seth and me, poetry became the means by which I saved my life. I stopped assembling; I discovered that I could bury in my writing the greater part of my pain and humiliation. The usefulness of poetry was revealed to me; all those poets had been telling the truth after all; anguish could be scooped up and dealt with. My loneliness could, by my secret gift of alchemy, be shaped into a less frightening form. I was going to survive—I soon saw that—and my survival was hooked into my quirky, accidental ability to put words into agreeable arrangements. I could even remake my childhood, that great void in which nothing had happened but years and years of shrivelling dependence. I wrote constantly and I wrote, as one critic said, "from the floor of a bitter heart."

And the irony, the treachery really, was that those who wrote critical articles on my books of poetry never—not one of them—distinguished between those poems I had written earlier and those that came later. (What grist for the Philistines who scoff at literary criticism.) To these critics my work was one arresting—"the arresting Charleen Forrest"—seamless whole. Which goes to show . . . .

Louis Berceau takes an enormous amount of sugar in his coffee. Four heaped teaspoons. I watch him—his hands are remarkably steady for a man of his age—dipping into the sugarbowl. The smiling girl of a waitress refills our cups several times, and Louis almost succeeds in emptying the bowl of sugar.

The mind is easily persuaded, a fact which Brother Adam mentioned in a recent letter, and Louis suddenly appears to me to be an altogether holy man sitting here stirring his sticky coffee. A monk. He inspires, in fact, a torrent of confession. In half an hour I have told him rather a lot about my marriage with Watson. He is an excellent listener, something I noticed yesterday in my mother's kitchen; he simply nods from time to time and fixes me with his opaque gaze. And out it all spills.

Watson, I tell him, was a man without a centre; he took on the colour of whichever landscape he happened to stumble across. Watson was a man who went to a Cary Grant movie and for a week after spoke in a light, slight, cocky English accent. He also did a weary, sneery Richard Widmark and—his favourite—a lean, mean, sinewy Dane Clark. Watson was a bit like a snake—the comparison is not really a good one for it suggests malice—but he was like a snake in his ability to continually shed his skin. Louis nods, and I hesitate, remembering that Louis too is a man who has shed his skin.

No, not like a snake, I correct myself, but like an actor who plays a number of roles one after the other, roles which he takes up energetically but later, with a kind of willful amnesia, shakes off and denies. Louis looks puzzled, and I try to explain. Watson's first incarnation I can only theorize about: he must have been a sort of child prodigy hatched into an otherwise undistinguished Scarborough family, bringing home to his bus-driver father and seamstress mother miraculous report cards and brimming with a kind of juicy, pedantic, junior-sized zeal. But by the time I met him, he had left that scrubbed good-son image behind and transformed himself into a studied, lazy dreamer of a student, tenderly anarchic, determinedly bumbling and odd. Oh, very, very odd. A structured oddity, though, which both thrilled and terrified him; he needed someone, me, to bring reality to the role. Later, as a married graduate student in Vancouver he had stunned me with a whole new set of mannerisms and attitudes; he literally fought his way into all-roundedness—he boxed, he ran for elections, he wrote articles on alfalfa, he signed petitions, he played softball, he even forced himself to attend chamber music recitals and read up on the history of ballet. And I had adored his earnestness, his determination, his rabid certainty which completed, it had seemed to me, some need of my own. I had not quite loved his Young Professor Self, his two year retreat—it seemed longer—into piped and bearded tolerant middle-class academe, his almost British equanimity, the completely unforeseen manner in which he began to utter whole networks of archaisms, words like vouchsafe and gainsay, words strung together with a troubling catgut of hitherto's, wheretofor's and whilst's; once, completely unabashed, he began a sentence with a burbling I daresay. It had been during that period that we actually bought a house with a garden. And actually conceived, with brooding deliberation, a child. House, wife, child, all he needed was the ivy. But already he was on his way to his next creation: rebellious young intellectual. For a while he did a balancing act between the two roles: one Sunday afternoon, sulky and depressed, the three of us had taken a walk around the neighbourhood. Seth, who must have been two years old at the time, walked between us, holding on to our hands. He was a little slow and unsteady, and Watson yanked him now and then angrily. But then we happened to pass by a house where an elderly couple were taking the afternoon sun. Seeing them, Watson had smiled gaily; he had swung Seth merrily to his shoulders in gruff fatherly fashion, crooning nonsense into his startled ears; this extraordinary display of affection had lasted until we were out of sight of the couple. Watching him, I had been sickened; that was when I knew he was a man without a centre.

As he careened toward thirty, he seemed to dissolve and reform with greater frequency, and each reincarnation introduced a new, more difficult strain of madness. Watson seemed unable, psychologically unable, physiologically unable, to resist any new current of thought. He was the consummate bandwagon man. Yet, I had loved him through most of his phases. Riding off to Vancouver on the back of his motorcycle, my face pressed for thousands of jolting miles into the icy smooth leather of his shoulders, hadn't I thought that I would be safe forever? And for most of the eight years we were together I tried to be tolerant, sometimes even enthusiastic. But what I could never accept was the way in which he coldly shut the door on his past lives. The fact that he so seldom wrote to his parents was a troubling warning; I could sympathize, but still it seemed heartless not to acknowledge the birthday gifts of knitted gloves and homemade fruitcake. Friends, abandoned along the way, wrote imploring letters—what is the matter with Watson, why doesn't he write or phone? The *Journal* which he founded in a burst of professional ardour became another dead end. He and Doug Savage quarrelled irrevocably over the definition and degree of scientific responsibility. And he refused to have anything to do with the Freehorns after they once teased him about his intermittent vegetarianism. Seth he regarded as a kind of recrimination, a remnant of a former, now shameful, life which he wanted to forget. Of course I saw that eventually I too would have to go.

"So it wasn't such a shock," Louis says, "when he . . . when you separated."

"It was still a shock," I tell him. "I knew it was coming, but I couldn't believe it when it actually happened."

When I look at snapshots of myself taken during that period I am amazed that I am not deformed by unhappiness, that I am not visibly disfigured, bent over and shredded with grief. In fact, except for my bitter, lime-section mouth, I look astonishingly healthy. In the first months I was so weighted with sorrow and relief that I slept twelve hours every night. I was so emptied out that I ate greedily and constantly, buying for myself baskets of fruit as though I were an invalid. My eyes in those photographs gleam like radium; perhaps I was crazed by the cessation of love, still disbelieving, always certain that Watson would return in another guise.

And in an entirely hopeless way I know I am still half-expecting him to turn up, remorseful, shriven, redeemed. Why else am I keeping Eugene waiting if not for my poor bone of expectation? Waiting has become my daily religion. Tomorrow I must remember to ask Brother Adam why, after all these years, I am still wearing my four-dollar wedding band.

When Louis speaks again, he asks with phlegm-plugged caution the perfect question. "Where is your Watson Forrest living now?"

One lives for moments like this. "Here," I pronounce solemnly, feeling my tongue cooling in delicious irony. "Watson lives right here. Isn't that amazing, Louis? Can you believe it? He lives here in this very town."

Louis shows perhaps a lesser degree of astonishment than I would like, but nevertheless he shakes his head in slow, grinning wonder.

And both of us, sitting in silence over our coffee cups are stewing in the rarified, blood-racing excitement of knowing exactly what will happen next.

❧

The Whole World Retreat is two and a half miles south-east of Weedham, reached by a neglected section of secondary road. The young-brown-eyed waitress at the Wayfarers' Inn is pleased to give us directions. "We buy all our lettuce and onions from them," she dimples, "and I don't care what anyone says about them, they make the best whole-wheat bread you ever tasted. Sort of nutty like, you know what I mean. Crunchy. All our customers ask where we get it."

We take the road slowly, swerving here and there to avoid potholes still glittering with yesterday's downpour. The countryside is green and rolling like calendar country; and the farms, though small, seem prosperous with good straight fences, herds of healthy cows and cheerful country mail boxes: The Mertins, Russell K. Anderson and Son, Bill and Hazel Rodman, Dwayne Harshberger, and, at last, a mail box that announces in blocky, green letters, The Whole World Retreat. Louis pulls the car to a stop on the shoulder of the road.

Back at the restaurant we agreed that we would simply drive past the place. It would be fun—I had emphasized the word *fun*, while despising the sound of it—it would be fun, out of curiosity, to drive by and see what the place looked like. I had proposed this to Louis in my lightest, most floating accents, as though this were no more than a crazy whim, a mad impulse, as though I were one of those programmed eccentrics who love to do mad, mad, mad things on the spur of the moment. Like Greta Savage who spends her life crouched on the contrived lip of unreason with her: *who else does crazy things like eat sardines for breakfast, who else is mad enough to take a holiday in Repulse Bay, who else is demented enough to tune in everyday to the Archers.* I have long suspected that her insanity is partly an affectation; now I adopt her shrill cry—"I know it sounds silly, Louis, but let's, just for the fun of it, drive by."

An act of adolescence, for don't high school girls in love with their math teachers furtively seek out their houses so they can cycle by, half-drowning in the illicit thrill of proximity. I hate Louis to see this undeveloped,

157

irrational side of my personality which hungers for cheap drama, but not enough to pass up the opportunity of seeing the Whole World Retreat. And besides, hasn't something more than chance brought me this close? Isn't there at least a suggestion of predestination in this afternoon's events, and hasn't Louis with his surprise revelation introduced a note of compelling, almost mystical significance? This day clearly has not been designed for rationality. Even though it is almost four o'clock, it does not seem right to turn back toward Scarborough where the tunafish casserole awaits, no doubt about it, already browning in my mother's oven, and where my mother herself waits with her contained, wordless questioning. Something entirely unforeseen has been set into action; I can feel the piping tattoo of my pulse in my throat, and, looking sideways at Louis's suddenly brightened eyes, I can see that he shares at least a measure of my excitement.

Beside the mail box a sign in heavy lettering announces: Green onions, Rhubarb, Homemade Bread, Fresh Eggs, Nursery Plants. And at the bottom in larger letters: Absolutely No Chemical Fertilizers. Louis and I sit, thoughtful for a moment, reading the sign and thinking our thoughts.

The house itself is set well back from the road. It is a top-heavy house, late Victorian in old-girlish brick, and its porch skirt of turned, white spindles gives it a blithe knees-up-Mother-Brown gaiety. Red and yellow tulips, not quite open, stand cheerful in a curved bed. The sloping front lawn is exceptionally beautiful with its twilled, gabardine richness and its fine finish of new growth.

There is no one in sight.

"They sell nursery plants," I remark to Louis.

"Yes," he says, "they do."

"I wonder what kind of things they have at this time of year."

"Hmmm."

"Actually," I take a deep breath, "actually I'd thought of buying some nursery plants."

No response from Louis.

I try again. "For you, Louis, the two of you. Something for the backyard. I thought it might make a good wedding gift."

More silence, and then Louis says cheerfully, "The perfect thing."

"We could just see what they have in stock."

"Are you . . . that is . . . are you sure?"

I pause. Then lunge. "Yes. I'm sure."

We leave the car—Louis checks both doors to make sure they are locked—and walks up the loose-gravelled drive toward the house. He stumbles slightly, then catches himself, but I don't even turn my head. I can feel excitement leaking in through my skin and for an instant I feel I might faint.

Up close the house looks slightly less picturesque. There is an old wringer washing machine on the porch, a pair of men's work gloves hanging on a nail (Watson's gloves?), two rain-sodden cartons of empty pop bottles. The screen door, rather rusty, has been inexpertly patched.

I knock.

"Hang on a minute," a woman's low voice calls from the shadows behind the screen, "I'm coming."

From inside the house we hear a young baby wailing. Baby! It takes my brain an instant to decode the message: a baby, oh God. Then plunging grief—Watson's baby. And in another instant I will be seeing Watson. He will come striding through that screen door and see me standing here with my old, grotesque vulnerability hanging around me like a hand-me-down raincoat. What am I doing here?

A young woman, plumply tranquil, wearing granny

glasses, pushes open the door. She wears a dirty, pink shirt over her jeans and on her hip rides a screaming, naked baby of about fifteen months. "Sorry to keep you waiting," she says in a flat but friendly southern Ontario voice. "I had the baby on the pot."

"That's all right," Louis says wheezing.

"What a lovely baby," I half moan . "Is it—" I peer closely, "Oh, it's a little girl."

"Faith," the woman says.

"Pardon?"

"Faith. That's her name."

Louis receives this information silently. He is searching his pockets for a handkerchief. Automatically, never missing a beat, my kindness act uncoils itself. "What an interesting name."

"My husband calls her Mustard Seed."

"Oh!" The word husband pierces me. "Oh?"

"Just a joke. Faith of a mustard seed. From the Bible."

"Oh, yes," my head bobs.

"Well," she says smiling and shifting the still wailing baby to her other hip, "is there anything I can help you with?"

"We saw your sign," Louis says indistinctly. His asthma is threatening; he is alarmingly tired. I should never have dragged him here; we should never have come.

"Nursery plants," I say, clearing my throat. "We were interested in nursery plants."

"Terrific," the young mother beams. (Young! she can't be older than twenty-five. I am shaken by a shower of dizzy shame for Watson, this is too much.)

"I wanted to buy something for a wedding gift," I say. "A shrub, I thought, something like that."

"Just a sec," the woman says. She peers over her

shoulder into the kitchen. "My husband can show you what we've got. Of course, it's early, there's not much, but he can at least show you what we've got."

"Look," I say, taking a step backwards, "we'll come back another time. When you've got more in."

She won't stop smiling at me; her yeasty good cheer glints off her glasses, making creamy Orphan Annie coins of her eyes. "You might as well have a look," she says. "He's right here. He'll be glad to show you what we've got."

Footsteps across the kitchen floor, a man's footsteps, a man's muffled pleasant voice saying, "I'm coming." *Watson.*

But the face which appears in the doorway isn't Watson; it is younger, leaner; it has blue eyes. And this man is taller. Not only that but he has straight, straw-coloured hair hanging to his shoulders and a muscular chest moving under his T-shirt. "How do you do," he says, stepping onto the porch.

"How do you do," Louis and I chorus. Louis gives me a quick, quizzing look, and I manage to flash him the smallest of smiles.

"Hey," the young man says, squinting at me, "hey, aren't you Charleen Forrest?"

Run, I cry, bolt. Now. Make for the road. Leap in the car, run. "Yes," I say, "I am."

"Well, for Pete's sake," the smiling girl says, showing a place in her lower jaw where a tooth is missing.

"Can you beat that," her husband mutters with awesome gentleness. The baby stops whimpering and holds herself suddenly rigid. Then she wets herself; a surprisingly wide stream of pale baby pee creams off her mother's hip and splashes to the porch floor.

"Oh hell," the girl says with equanimity, stepping sideways out of the puddle.

161

"Charleen Forrest," her husband murmurs again. He sends me a warm, slow smile.

"How do you know who I am?" I ask, thinking: Watson, he must keep a picture of me, imagine that, who would have thought it of Watson?

"I've got all your books," he says. "And your picture's on the back. I would have recognized you anywhere."

"Oh," I say, disappointed.

"And then, of course, knowing Watson—" he shrugs and smiles, "not that that matters. We really dig your stuff. Cheryl and I."

"That's for sure," Cheryl says.

"Thank you," I say absurdly. Sweetly?

"Don't suppose you've seen Watson lately?" he asks me.

I stare.

"We sure miss him," Cheryl says in tones soft with regret. "It's just not the same here without Watson. Is it, Rob?"

"He was a beautiful guy," Rob says mournfully. "One real beautiful guy, that's all I can say."

"But look," I say to the two of them in a sharply raised voice, "he still lives here? Doesn't he?"

"Gosh, no," the gap-toothed Cheryl says. "Gee, it's been—what Rob?—two years now?"

"Yeah. More than two years. He split—let's see—it was round the end of March, wasn't it, Cheryl? Two years ago March. We haven't had a postcard from him even."

"But that's impossible," I tell them firmly. "It can't be true."

A look of concern passes between them, a look which firmly shuts me out, and I feel a nudge of suspicion. Are they trying to protect Watson, pretending he isn't here, trying to fool me like this?

"You see," Rob says, taking the baby from his wife, "Watson sort of, well, I guess you could say he got disenchanted. You know, with the whole scene, the whole group thing, what we were trying to do here."

"And the others," Cheryl prompts him.

He nods. "That was part of it too, I guess. There were about eight of us, Cheryl and me and the others. All of them younger than Watson. Mostly kids who'd dropped out of the whole city thing. Younger kids. Watson kept saying they were getting younger and younger all the time. He finally got to thinking, I guess, that it was time to move on to another scene."

"He was forty," I tell them abruptly. "Two years ago he had his fortieth birthday. In March."

"Gee," Cheryl says, "Forty!"

"But he must be here," I insist, "because every month he sends me a cheque from here. The child support money. For our son. He sends it every month. Always right on the fifteenth and it comes from here. Weedham. I know because I always check the postmark."

They laugh softly as if I'd said something outlandishly amusing. "That's Rob," Cheryl explains grinning. "Rob's the one who sends off the cheque."

"You mail me the cheque?" I ask dazed.

"It was the one thing Watson wanted me to do. He left, Christ, I don't know how many postdated cheques. Enough 'til the boy's eighteen, I think, isn't it Cheryl?"

"And enough money in the bank to cover them. That's what's important, I guess, eh?"

Rob continues, "He wrote a note, left it on the back-door, this door here. All about the cheques, like where to send them and all. And I haven't forgotten one, not so far anyways."

"That's very kind of you," I say, feeling my mouth freeze with etiquette and sorrow.

"But you know," Rob rambles on, "I might forget sometime. Memory's not my strong point, ask Cheryl here. What I should do, since you're standing right here, is just give you the whole bunch of cheques. Right now. That way you'd have them right with you and you could just cash them as the dates roll round."

Cheryl nods enthusiastically at this piece of logic, and I feel suddenly flattened by confusion. Something inside me twists, something sour, something sharp, but I manage to smile and say, "Sure. Why not? While I'm here I might as well take them with me."

Cheryl goes into the house and comes back in a minute with a large brown envelope. "They're in here. You can count them if you want."

"That's okay," I say. "I don't have to count them. And thank you."

"No need to thank us," Rob says. And then he adds wistfully, "We sure miss Watson. It's not the same."

Should I ask them? I have to. "Where's Watson living now?"

"East," Rob says. "He went east."

"You mean the Maritimes?"

He laughs again. "No, not geographical east. Philosophical east. He was into the mysticism thing. Hindu mainly.

"Buddha too," Cheryl offers.

"You don't know where he went?" I can hear a shameful pleat in my voice. "Geographically, I mean?"

"No. Like I said, we haven't heard anything from Watson. Not in two years. Just that note stuck on the door. He didn't say where he was going, just that he was going East. With a capital E. East."

"And that's all?"

"That's all. The others, they kind of drifted off one by one too. After the baby was born. Some of them couldn't

164

really ride with the baby thing. So now there's just Cheryl and me. And Mustard Seed here." He blows a noisy kiss into the baby's fat neck. "We're just kind of a family now, you might say. We still do some farming but not like when Watson was here. But our bread baking operation is going along pretty well."

"And the nursery plants," Cheryl adds.

"Oh, yeah, the nursery plants. That's what you folks were looking for, wasn't it?"

Behind the greenhouse in the spilled, late afternoon sunlight, Louis and I pick out some good healthy shrubs: six mock orange with their roots bound in sacking. And a flat of petunias, white and pink mixed. I pay Rob with a twenty-dollar bill, and he helps Louis put them in the trunk of the car. Then we shake hands all around and head for home.

I sit beside Louis with the brown envelope on my lap and it occurs to me that I will never again receive a message from Watson, Watson my lapsed-bastard, first-love, phantom husband. The last link—a smudged, treasonous postmark— has just been taken away from me. It wasn't much, but it was better than nothing. The arrival of Watson's cheques—the regularity, the suppressed silence—offered me something: not hope, certainly not hope, I am not such a fool as that, but a pencil line of connecting sense in the poor tatter I'd made of my life. A portion of renewal. And a means by which the worth of other things might be tested. Damn you, Watson.

"There, there," Louis is saying. "There, there now." The curving kindness of his voice—what a good man he is—makes me conscious of the tears falling out of my eyes.

Chapter 6

It takes us a long time to get back to Scarborough. For twenty minutes we're stalled in traffic. An accident maybe; it could be anything. So many people in this city. Louis's cautious driving style, so reassuring earlier in the day, is an irritant now that it's five-thirty, five-forty-five, six o'clock. A heavy rug of sky pushes down on the streaked sunlight; my head aches. At exactly six-thirty my mother will be placing her Pyrex casserole on the blue, crocheted hotpad in the middle of the kitchen table. I twitch with nerves. Doesn't Louis know how punctual my mother is about meals? Well, he'll soon learn.

Louis tries to cheer me up by talking about his favourite poet, Robert Service. I wish he wouldn't. *Please, Louis, don't.* His voice cracks with strain and it's disappointing to hear he hasn't read Hopkins. But his lips smack with pleasure over a stanza of "The Shooting of Dan McGrew," and I chide myself for expecting more than I deserve.

At last Scarborough, the shopping centre, the school where I went to kindergarten (I was the one whose socks were always sliding down), the grid of streets so minutely familiar but whose separate names now seem cunningly elusive. At seven o'clock Louis pulls up in front of the house, and from the living room window a face (whose?) registers our return.

"Aren't you coming in, Louis?" I ask. "Aren't you staying for supper?"

"I'm a little tired," he says weakly. "This chest of mine."

"Are you sure you won't come in? Just for a minute?"

"I think I'll have an early night," he says. "You'll explain to your mother, won't you?"

"Sure."

"I'll bring over the shrubs in the morning. Put them in first thing in the morning."

"Fine. And Louis . . . thanks for everything." I emphasize the word everything; suddenly I'm tired, too.

"Good night."

"Good night."

I'm late. Will my mother dare to scold me. Yes, she won't be able to help herself. This in itself is alarming enough, but something else is even more frightening, something unnatural about the crouched, waiting house, or is it that strange car parked in front? Or perhaps there are such things as psychic waves, perhaps Greta Savage is right after all about telepathic electricity, perhaps tense, waving vibrations actually penetrate my skin as I walk around to the back door. I don't know. But coming into this house alone at this hour makes me suddenly and ridiculously weak with fear.

The first thing I see in the kitchen is my mother's tuna fish casserole. Its tender breadcrumb crust is unbroken. A serving spoon lies tentatively by its side, but the table hasn't been set. How odd.

Eugene. What is he doing here? He is supposed to be at the Orthodontists' banquet eating warmed-up roast beef and hard little scoops of mashed potato. He crosses the kitchen and presses me in his arms. Eugene, not here, really, can't you see my mother's standing right here?

My mother is standing by the stove. Her hands can't seem to find a resting place. They're not clutched behind her back, they're not clenched at her hips, not folded across her chest, not nervously laced beneath her chin; they are floating freely in a frightening pantomime of helplessness.

Martin and Judith. They are standing in the doorway. How curious, they aren't actually touching each other, so why do they seem to swim before me in blurry tandem unison like synchronized dancers. Married people grow to look alike—it must be true—just look at those two twin jaws slung in the same attitude of guarded concern. Concern? What is the matter with them?

And then there are the two policemen. Why do policemen wear that dispirited shade of blue, snow-shovel blue, looseleaf notebook blue? Two policemen sitting at the kitchen table. Sitting there. But when I come in the door, they shuffle politely to their feet. A dream, of course.

"Charleen," Eugene holds me close.

"Thank heavens you're home," Judith's mordant contralto escapes in a gasp.

"Now don't get excited, Judith," Martin says. "Give her a minute, everyone."

"Are you Mrs. Forrest?" one of the policemen demands.

"Wouldn't you like to go into the living room?" my mother frets.

"You must be calm," Eugene says into my shoulder. "You must try to remain calm."

"And your regular domicile is Vancouver?"

"Just take it easy, take it easy now."

"Keep things in proportion . . ."

"You'll find the living room more comfortable."

"We have one or two questions for you, Mrs. Forrest."

"Here, Charleen, sit down. Martin, get her to sit down."

"You'd better sit down; you must sit down."

"There, that's better isn't it?"

"And when was your departure from Vancouver, Mrs. Forrest?"

"Leave her alone for Christ's sake, can't you see she's confused."

"Take it easy, Char, take it easy—"

" . . . if you'll just answer a few questions . . ."

"The living room is cooler and you could . . ."

"Keep your balance, that's the important . . ."

"Your exact arrival in Toronto was . . .?"

"Hey, give her a chance . . ."

"You tell her."

"I'm only trying to help."

"I think Eugene should be the one. He's . . ."

"We understand this is upsetting, Mrs. Forrest . . ."

"The living room . . ."

" . . . unfortunately they expect a complete report at headquarters."

"Charleen, listen to me. Are you listening?"

"Yes." Was that my voice? Was it?

Eugene is sitting next to me with both my hands in his and he is saying the most preposterous things. Incredible things. How melodramatic—I wouldn't have thought it of Eugene. Seth has disappeared, Eugene is saying that Seth has disappeared. What a joke. Is it a joke? It can't be because these policemen are writing things down and besides my mother doesn't like jokes. And neither, I realize for the first time in my life, neither do I.

Seth has been taken somewhere by Greta Savage. Taken away. Several days ago. No one knows for sure when. Or how. But they have both been missing for several days. Now don't get excited. No one knows where they are at this precise moment, but in all probability they are safe. Greta Savage has disappeared with my son and Doug Savage has called in the police, that is what has happened, Charleen.

"Say something, Charleen," Eugene commands.

"Is she going to faint?" Judith's arm is on my shoulder.

"It looks like it. Someone get some water."

"Are you going to faint, Charleen?"

"Darling."

"No," I say distinctly. "No, I'm not going to faint."

❧

All I have to do is hold on to consciousness. Nothing is more important than that, for the moment nothing more is required of me. But if I shut my eyes for even a second I will never see Seth again. I must sit still, I must pretend I am composed of dry, unjointed wood, if I move one inch from this table there will be an explosion.

I must try to understand. Slowly, perfectly like a child memorizing the Twenty-third Psalm, *He restoreth my soul for his something-or-other sake.* Certain facts must be absorbed.

Doug Savage has been trying to reach me all day. The last call came from Parry Sound. He phoned at least four times today. Finally he agreed to talk to Judith. Judith phoned downtown immediately and had Eugene paged at the conference. Eugene came home at once and since then he has been trying unsuccessfully to reach Doug Savage. But Doug Savage promised Judith he would phone back at eight o'clock. That's less than an hour, Judith says, only fifty minutes now, and until then there is nothing anyone can do.

Seth and Greta have been missing all week. While I was eating English muffins on the train, while I was kissing Eugene in the back of a taxi and, Oh God, while I was chasing around the countryside with Louis Berceau on a foolish, pointless, private, childish quest Greta and Seth disappeared; they took the Savages' car in the middle of the night—there is some confusion about which night it was, Sunday? Monday? The Vancouver police think—there is reason to believe—that Greta may have given Seth some sleeping pills. Sleeping pills!

For the first two days Doug thought he could avoid calling in the police. He had a hunch that Greta might have taken Seth to a cottage they own in the mountains in Alberta. He borrowed a car and drove all night, but when he got there, he found only rumpled beds and tire tracks. They must have spent the first night there. After that, he thought they might have gone to Winnipeg where Greta has old friends, but when he got there, twenty-four hours later, he couldn't find any trace of her. So he phoned here last night— Can that possibly have been only last night?—hoping Greta had made some kind of contact; after that he phoned the police. There had been no alternative.

The police: they are looking right across the country, but they have to move cautiously (are they dealing with a mad woman?). They don't know. I don't know. The situation has been judged too risky for public appeals, but they are making all sorts of inquiries. It seems Greta is driving mostly at night. A gas station attendant just outside Thunder Bay is almost certain they stopped there: a woman and boy resembling the police description stopped for gas and a hamburger. Did the woman appear dangerous? No. Had the boy appeared intimidated or drugged? No one had noticed. Which way were they headed? The attendant wasn't sure. All he could remember was that they were in a hurry.

❧

There is nothing to do but wait until Doug calls again.

The two police officers wait courteously in the living room. My mother frets about whether or not to offer them coffee. Eventually she decides against it. She is more confused than alarmed; her six-thirty supper has been disrupted and in some indefinable way the untouched casserole precludes the making of coffee. As always she is just outside of events, hovering—ghostlike but demanding—at the perimeter. "How could you leave him with people like that?" she scolds me sharply. "What kind of friends are they?"

Judith tries to soothe her, but Martin flushes with anger. Martin is convinced that what I need is a stiff drink, but of course there is nothing, not in this house. "I've got some Scotch in my suitcase," he says, suddenly assertive. He brings it out, and my mother, her hands still flapping wildy, finds a juice glass. But my stomach leaps and dissolves; I can't even look at it; Martin picks up the glass, regards it mildly, and then drinks it off neat.

Judith's voice floats over my head in a sort of chanting reassuring descant. "Look at it like this, Charleen, they've both been seen alive and well. Yesterday. So they're okay. Maybe she's a bit on the crazy side, but she isn't dangerous, that's what Doug Savage said on the phone. He said try not to get Charleen upset because Greta wouldn't hurt a fly, it's just a matter of hours before they find him."

Martin pats me awkwardly on the crown of my head. "Look here now, Charleen, she's a little unbalanced maybe, but, God, who isn't, and you've known her for years. You know she wouldn't do anything to hurt him, nothing *really* crazy. You've got to keep thinking what she's really like."

Eugene sits wordless beside me. He's not a wordy man, he never was a wordy man. He's still holding on to

172

my hands, and I'm grateful to him. There's nothing to say. And nothing we can do.

I think of the huge distance between Toronto and Vancouver, the blending agricultural regions, the mountain ranges, river systems, squares of acreage, contours, city limits, county lines, townships and backyards with chickens and shrubs and children. I try to hold that whole terrain in my head; it is a numbing exercise, though it shouldn't be all that difficult, for haven't I just crossed that country myself? Haven't I touched every inch of it? I think of all the people strung out over that distance, imbedded in their separate time zones. Seven-thirty: they're washing dishes. I can hear cutlery right across the country dropping into drawers. They're bathing children, playing bridge, reading newspapers, all of them magically sealed in their preserving spheres of activity. Out there in all that darkness is Greta's car, a blue Volvo—it has to be there—cruising past apartment houses and suburbs and farms; and these people, shutting their windows, watering their lawns, walking their dogs, they just *allow* her to go by. Maybe they even wave to her. Maybe she waves back, she has always been so friendly, so pathetically friendly. She would do anything to help a friend; she is so kind, she wouldn't hurt a fly. Remember that, above all remember that; she wouldn't hurt a fly.

❧

Eight o'clock. We wait in the kitchen. The silence is minutely detailed like a blueprint for a piece of immensely complicated machinery. The minutes are sharply cornered and pressing, and each one hangs rigidly separate.

Eight-fifteen. Why doesn't Doug call? Something has happened. One of the policemen asks if he might phone in a report.

"No," I gasp.

Eugene shakes his head, "Better not tie up the phone here." The policeman nods politely and asks if he might use the next-door neighbour's phone.

At this my mother looks up, horribly alarmed, and I see her mouth twist into its tight diminishing shape. I know that shape, its denials, negations, interdictions, the way it closes to inquiries, the way it forbids, the way it ultimately blames and refuses. Now. She is going to do it now, going to give one of her terrible, unforgiving no's.

But she doesn't. Bewilderment—or is it fatigue?— makes her thin lips collapse. She nods a shaky assent. Then she rises and puts the kettle on.

In a moment the policeman returns; there are no further developments, he tells us. We will have to wait a little longer, that's all.

My mother is moving around the kitchen putting her trembling hands to work. (What have I done to her, what have I done to her this time?) Now she is making tea, now she is arranging jittery cups on a tray. Judith gets up to help her and together they begin to make sandwiches. How extraordinary, my mother actually has a package of boiled ham in the refrigerator. And cheese. Sandwiches are disaster fare; who would have thought my mother had a sense of occasion. She and Judith stand with their backs to us buttering bread. They are exactly the same height; I never noticed that. Their elbows move together, marionettes on a single lateral string. Abstract kinship suddenly made substantial. But why am I thinking about ham and cheese and kinship? Why am I not thinking about the centre of this disaster; why am I not thinking about Seth?

Because I can't bear to.

Seth dead. No, that's not possible. It's not possible because my life isn't possible without him; it's not possible when I'm sitting here, wired with reality. Pulse, heartbeat, nerves, breath, sudden sweating, hurting consciousness, all the signs of life failing me now by *not* failing. In this kitchen every small sound is magnified; my mother's half-invalid, half-despairing shuffle, the policemen laughing in the living room (laughing!), Martin crashing into his ham sandwich, the sugar spoon which strikes with dead neutrality on the formica table. And my eyes: suddenly I can see with wolfish clarity. I can see the neat hem on my mother's sheer kitchen curtains, her tiny over and under and over stitches, and through the curtains a glittering, mocking, glassware moon is coming into view. Evening. Nine o'clock. Doug Savage, why doesn't he phone? Seth dead. No, it's not possible.

Sleeping pills. Greta stuffing Seth with sleeping pills; she is so small, such a weak, wiry woman, something dark about her face, always a sense of shadow. But Seth is quite strong for his age, well developed, remarkably healthy. His health is startling; something godlike nourishes him despite his inheritance; I've never been able to understand it. I picture his strength against Greta's weakness, and a tiny flashbulb of hope goes off under my skin; she can't possibly harm him.

Then I remember how clever she is, how she is veined with a wily unaccountability. Her secrecy about Watson's letters; she hints she has heard from him but says nothing more. And her sudden, piercing, illogical bursts of purity. Madness? Not really madness. How did Doug once put it to me? "Greta is rational enough, it's just that her rationality is not as evenly distributed as it is in more balanced people." Certainly she is not a fanatic, not in the accepted sense of that word, but she suffers from blinding pinpricks of virtue. The way, for instance, she once burned Doug's thesis on the diseases of short ferns because she believed it had been conceived to fill an artificial academic requirement. (Only by good fortune had she overlooked the carbon.)

Her weaving too is girded by purity; the way she refuses to touch synthetics and swears to give up weaving altogether if she is forced to work with wool which is chemically dyed and treated. Then there is her violent anti-smoking stance. And her contempt for Eugene and what she considers his crass profession. Her leaps into various systems of the human potential movement. Her bright, birdlike fixations: the insistence (I suddenly remember) with which she had determined to pick up Seth at school last week. Then there is her refusal to have children; here perhaps her fanaticism is grounded on objectivity, for she would have made a shocking mother for all her devotion to Seth. But most painful to me has always been her clinging admiration for Watson; she once confided in an orgy of tactlessness that she "reverenced" Watson's decision to alter his life. She keeps track of him with passionate persistence, long after everyone else has given up, smothering him with letters, forcing him to acknowledge her existence, coercing him by her indefatigable energy to keep her supplied with news of his latest incarnations. Ah, Greta, poor Greta, poor, twisted, buggered-up Greta, where are you? It's nine-thirty and I'm going crazy, where are you?

❧

In the living room the policemen have turned on the television. Hawaii Five-O. Screams, sirens, the sound of bullets, throaty accusations, weeping, all so bearably unreal. What a poor tissue fiction is, how naively selective and compressed and organized, justice redressed in exactly sixty calculated minutes, the violence always just marginally tolerable, the pressure just within the

176

bounds of human acceptance, tragedy in an airtight marketable tin.

Martin paces. My mother and Judith wash plates and cups, and Eugene goes next door to phone a car rental firm. He has decided that the minute Seth is located we must have a car to get to him.

I think bitterly of Watson. Wherever he is, he is being spared this hour. Of everything he has left undone as a father this seems the worst.

Even Louis—I think of him with a flash of envy—even Louis in his furnished room, so wonderfully protected from all this. So innocently unaware. What peace not to know.

And Brother Adam, you with your abstract wisdom, your fire-escape view, you know nothing of what I'm suffering, you are a dream, you don't even exist for me now.

And Seth, what are you thinking, wherever you are? Are you safe?

❧

Judith, always compulsive, is tidying the kitchen. She covers the tunafish casserole with a dinner plate and puts it in the refrigerator. Then she swirls a wet cloth over the table, picking up my purse and putting it on top of the cupboard.

"What's this?" she asks, picking up an envelope.

I am slow to react; am I losing consciousness after all? Then I say, "Oh. That's mine."

It is the envelope containing the child support cheques, my last connection with Watson. A business envelope, eight-by-eleven in business-coloured brown. Closed with a huge paperclip.

I open it idly, and the cheques slide out on my lap. What a lot of cheques, twelve for each year, and yes—I count them—enough to last until Seth's eighteenth birthday. And a stack of addressed envelopes with a rubber band around them. There's even a sheet of postage stamps. How wonderfully organized of Watson, beneath his many layers he must still be in touch with that boy prodigy of his youth and with his dull parents who always paid their bills, in touch too with his unknown, sober ancestors who never ran away from their debts.

There is something different about the final cheque: it is dated for Seth's eighteenth birthday, May 21, and it is made out for five thousand dollars. Five thousand dollars! I feel my breath harden; how had Watson managed to save five thousand dollars? He must have been exceedingly careful over the years to save that much money. But how pointless, how useless, a piece of paper for a son who is missing. A son who can't be found.

I can't help it. I'm starting to cry. I can't help it. This piece of paper, this five thousand dollars—it isn't enough. It's so futile, it's just like Watson to make a gesture like this, so stagey, so impressive and so utterly, utterly useless.

But there's something else in the envelope. Still crying I pull it out. It's another piece of paper, a page raggedly torn from a notebook. But the message on it is carefully typed.

I have to read it twice before I realize what it is. It is Watson's farewell note, the one he must have stuck on the screen door before he left the Whole World Retreat. Rob and Cheryl, those two good children, had been more than worthy of the trust he placed in them, guarding not only the cheques but his final words of good-bye. How absurd, though, to write a farewell note on a typewriter, how somehow incongruous, how like Watson. The note he once left me, the one I burned in the barbeque, that note had been typed too. I had forgotten Watson could type; I had forgotten a lot about Watson. But I had not forgotten his embarrassing penchant for prophecy; reading his words of good-bye, it all seems suddenly very familiar.

Dear Brothers and Sisters,
These words are written in love and sadness.
The life of the spirit is love
but it is also containment and peace.

It is time for me to leave you.
Time to go East.
You will understand.
Understanding is all.

Two things I ask of you.
First, care for the land which
We have made green.
It will feed you purely.
But the grass will give you
Peace and delight.
Care for the grass before the grain.

Secondly, I leave an envelope of envelopes.
Please mail one each month for me.
I put my faith in all of you.

Remember
There will be other lives
Other Worlds.
        Watson Forrest
         ❧

   At last the telephone is ringing. Eugene leads me to the hallway, holding my arm as though I were a thousand years old. Everyone—Martin, my mother, the two policemen—gather around me.

"Hello."

"Charleen."

"Doug."

"Are you all right?"

"What's happened? Have you found them?"

"No, but I think we're onto something now."

"Where are you?"

"I'm out at Weedham, Ontario with the cops. At the Whole World place."

"Yes?" I breathe.

"They said you were here—"

"Yes, but—"

"They're not here. But we haven't given up."

"Tell me," my voice bends with pleading. "do you think they're . . . all right?"

"Oh, God, Charleen, if you knew how terrible I feel about all this. You and Seth and . . . if you only knew. But I think it's going to be all right, I think we're going to find them."

• "What happened? Do you know what happened?"

"I just don't know. I thought Greta was okay on Sunday. A little edgy, but no worse than usual anyway. But as near as we can figure out, she overdid the meditation thing. She rounded. That's what we think. She just rounded."

"Rounded?"

"Went over . . . you know, over the top. It happens sometimes. She lost touch with the real world, what they call rounding. But I know she'll come around. You know Greta, she wouldn't hurt a—"

"But why did she take Seth?" I am crying into the phone. "Why did she have to take Seth?"

"We're not sure. That is, the police can't figure it out unless she was just crazy to have a kid of her own. But I tried to tell them I don't think that's it. I've got a crazy

180

hunch—this sounds really crazy—but I think maybe she's trying to take Seth to Watson."

"Watson?"

"I know it sounds insane, but you know Greta. She might take it into her head that Seth would be better off with Watson. You know how she idolized the guy, always has. And she was, well, a little uneasy in her mind about Eugene and all that, you know how she is sometimes . . ."

"You really think . . ."

"It's just a guess, that's all. That's why I came out here, out to Weedham. But the kids here haven't laid eyes on him for a couple of years."

"Greta is taking Seth to Watson?" I repeat this numbly.

"That's all I can think of. I'm going crazy trying to think. That's why I'm two hours late calling you. I turned my watch back instead of forward when the time zone changed, I just found out, that's how mixed up I am. I've just been looking and looking all week and I'm just about out of my mind."

"We'll find them," I say falteringly, unbelievingly.

"Look, I'm sure Greta knows where Watson's living. I mean, I know she writes to him now and then."

"Yes. I know."

"Look, Char, I don't suppose you've got any idea yourself where Watson might be."

I think for a quarter of a minute and then I say, "Yes."

I give Doug the address very slowly so he will be able to write it down.

❧

Standing in my mother's crowded little hall, we make hurried plans. Eugene and I and one of the policemen will go to the meeting point and wait for Doug Savage.

The police will send reinforcements immediately.

The other officer will stay here with the family. He has just received a message, he tells us a motel operator near Parry Sound reported renting a room last night to a middle-aged woman who was driving a dark coloured Volvo with B.C. plates. Was she alone? The report is not entirely clear, the officer explains. It was late at night, very dark, and no one is sure whether she was alone or not.

"We can take my car," Eugene says.

"Your car?" Martin asks.

"A rental," Eugene explains shortly. "They've just brought it over."

"God," Martin says, "that was quick." He says this with mingled surprise and admiration, and for a moment all of us turn and regard Eugene who is checking his wallet for his license. Such a simple thing, renting a car; Eugene would never be able to understand why my family stands in awe of such simple acts. I pick up my purse in the kitchen, and Eugene and I follow the policeman out the back door.

It is a big car, hugely clean, and the three of us fit in the front seat easily, Eugene driving, I in the middle, the policeman enthusiastically giving directions from the right. Eugene turns the car south toward the lake.

For me every passing car takes on extraordinary significance; each one must be checked off against Greta's blue Volvo. *She is sure to be in the city now.* I strain in the dark to see.

Vancouver, Calgary, Thunder Bay, Parry Sound, what could it signify? Perhaps a straight meaningless sweep across the whole country. What if they kept going, across Quebec, across the Maritimes, what if they dropped senseless into the sea like lemmings?

Then suddenly I am overcome with flooding despair. A moment ago, hearing the gassy zoom of the rented car I had felt temporarily buoyant. Now, from nowhere, comes the knowledge that Seth is dead. The certainty arrives in the middle of a breath. I had inhaled with hope and by the time my breath left me I was certain he was lost forever. This dark road, this silence.

It was a night like this when Seth was born. A spring night, the streets dry and dark with only a cold knot of a moon in the sky. Watson was out at a peace rally and I, drinking coffee in the apartment and feeling the first kick of pain, had been shocked and frightened and then, suddenly, for no reason, I had become serenely confident, packing quickly and neatly, phoning the doctor, locking the windows, calling the taxi, and then riding down the tree-arched Vancouver streets, sucking in the cool, friendly darkness as though it were somehow edible, exaltation knocking inside my heart. This was it, this was the beginning of my life, the only life that was going to matter.

"You want to take a left here," the officer advises Eugene after a mere ten minutes. "This is a one-way."

"Okay."

"Now, you want to jog right at the stop sign. I know this neighbourhood pretty well."

"Parking?"

"Anywhere now."

Eugene slows the car. "Maybe we'd better not park right in front of the building," he suggests.

"Squeeze in there by the hydrant, what the hell. Anyway there it is, that's the house. That big bugger on the left."

This is a certain type of Toronto street—narrow and, despite the streetlights, deeply shadowed. Cars park all along one side. The houses are tall and narrow and old; wooden porches hang on to their blackened brick fronts. It's a warm night, and here and there people are sitting out on their front steps; I can see the glowing red tips of their cigarettes. The front yards are small and, though I can't see in the dark, I know they are made up of packed earth and clumps of weeds; this is the kind of neighbourhood where there are always too many children and where it is shady even on the brightest days.

The blue flicker of television sets fills most of the front windows. Eugene turns off the ignition and says, "Let's go."

The policeman stands outside for a moment checking the other cars on the block. "That's one of ours," he says pointing to an unmarked Ford. "And those two guys are ours too."

"Let's go in," Eugene presses.

"But Doug Savage isn't here," I say, suddenly confused.

"They'll be a few minutes yet," the policeman says, checking his watch, "all the way from Weedham. Even in good traffic that's a fair run."

"No sign of a Volvo," I hear Eugene saying.

"She could've ditched it anywhere."

"I'll go in," I tell them.

"I wouldn't advise that," the policeman says, "you never know about these characters."

"I'm going in," I tell him again.

"I'll come with you," Eugene says.

"I think it would be better if I went alone, Eugene."

"We could back you up," the policeman says, thinking hard.

"If I could just talk to him alone. For a few minutes."

The policeman ponders a moment and then asks, "Is he, well you know him, he was your husband. What I mean, is he a dangerous guy?"

"Is he, Charleen?" Eugene turns to me.

"No," I almost smile. "He's not dangerous at all. He's like a . . . like . . . like a baby."

❧

The policeman checks with his friends in the parked car. When he comes back he nods at us and says, "Okay. We'll have a go."

It's a large house, one of the largest on the street, a three storey with jutting bays and ugly round-topped windows. Even in the dark I can see that it's in shocking condition. A few of the windows are broken, and most of them, except for two or three at the top, are dark. The front steps are shaky. The open porch is garishly lit by a naked bulb and it's filled with dirty plastic toys, a wicker chair with a rotted cushion, a dead plant in a pot. I'm frightened now, reluctant; perhaps I've made a crucial error in coming here.

The three of us stand on the porch for a moment, and for some reason the policeman is telling us about himself. His name is Bill Miller, he says, and he doesn't usually come out on jobs like this. He's filling in, he tells us, because this is a special case. Of course, he says shrugging, every case is special if you think about it. "We'll back you up," he says again in what sounds to me like Dragnet dialogue. "If your boy's up there, we'll get him out."

There are six doorbells stacked in a wiggly line on the door frame, but the name we want isn't there. A man appears in the doorway, a short, scrawny man, neither young nor old, with a rabbitty neck and a small, sharp nose. He is so drunk he has to lean on the door jamb to keep from falling down.

"Yeah?" he challenges us.

I explain whom we want to see.

"Sure, sure, he's up there," he tells us. "Lives at the

top. I told him I'd put up a lousy doorbell for him, but what the fuck for, no one ever comes to see him."

"Is there anyone up there with him now?" Eugene asks.

"Naw. 'Less they come up the fire escape. I been here all night."

Bill Miller says, "Look, mister, what we want to know is, did a woman come in here tonight?"

"Woman, eh?" he winks obscenely. "I always tell him that's what he needs, a good roll in the hay to straighten him out. He's a real nut."

"A woman with a boy?" Eugene asks carefully.

"Search me," he shrugs. "Why don't ya go up and have a look for yerself. Third floor. Name's on the door, ya can't miss."

Eugene and Bill Miller position themselves on the dark second floor landing. The stairway to the third floor is narrower and there is no railing, but a dim lightbulb shows the way.

I am at the top of the house standing in a tiny hall; there is only one door and it is clearly marked in blocky, hand-painted letters, The Priory, Bro. Adam. (The diminutive "Bro." is a warning.) Silence. Then the sound of my own breathing rushing out into the silence. I knock smartly on the door. Twice. Three times.

No answer, but through the old cracked wood I can hear something stirring. Like cloth being moved. Like someone sighing. Someone moaning.

I knock once more and wait. And then I turn the knob. It opens easily, a wide swinging, and I call out, "I'm coming in."

Afterwards I could hardly believe that I spent less than five minutes in that room. A small square room under the eaves, and yet my first impression was one of blinding, dazzling space. It was the mirrors, of course, huge mirrors mounted on two facing walls and lining the sloping ceiling, so that the small space seemed endless and unbelievably complex, like the sudden special openings that sometimes occur in dreams.

It was like stepping into the warm, glowing, artificial interior of a greenhouse with its combination of plant life, glinting glass and stillness. The air, after the reeking hallway, was deliciously fresh and smelled of earth and new growth. A narrow window let in the fragrant early spring air and on the other side a door stood open to an iron fire escape.

The room was alive with tiny lights. They were strung on wires and they beamed like miniature suns on the wooden flats of grass. The whole room, except for a neatly made-up army cot, was carpeted with grass. In the rebounding arrangements of mirrors and lights, the grass stretched endlessly, acres of it, miles of it; it was like coming upon a secret Alpine meadow, like a pocket of perfect and perpetual springtime where there was no night, no thought of cold or death. Even time seemed to fall away from me, as though the endless grass lived in another dimension altogether where growth and fertility took the place of hours and days.

Watson sat on the bed in a lotus position; I was conscious first of his gleaming skull and then of a certain bodily heaviness under his robe of dull red cloth. A book lay open on his lap. "I was afraid you might try to come," he said after a moment.

My throat closed soundless over his name: Watson, Watson, Watson. Still there, still there, that tender—no, no, more than tender—sliver of pain and youthful love lodged in the centre of my body. A twisting breathlessness like a rising funnel-shaped cloud of anguish pressed on my lungs, robbing me of speech and, for a moment, of coherence. What was I doing here leaning on this doorway, gasping for breath and for that portion of love that had surely died?

"Why are you here?" he asked again.

Then, like a stone sinking, I regained the powers of speech and thought.

"Brother Adam." I pronounced the words with finality, as though they were a summation. He gazed at me with detached calm.

"Brother Adam," I said again, deriving a curious energy from the flat sound of those two words. I couldn't summon surprise. I couldn't pretend surprise even to myself; nor could I distinguish the moment in time when I'd begun to know who Brother Adam might be. It seemed to me at that moment, standing in that incredible room, that I must always have known.

"You shouldn't have come," he said. (No, I shouldn't have. I had wanted a holy man with a bright prophetic eye and a tongue threaded with psalms, not this squatting, middle-aged would-be-sage grunting his way into being.) Of course Watson's vision of himself had never been less than apocalyptic: It occurred to me that the name Adam was just slightly substandard in its patent simplicity. A swindle really. Adam, king of his rooming-house Eden.

"There's something I have to ask you," I said firmly.

"I'm leaving tomorrow."

"Where?"

"East. I'm going East."

I came close to smiling, for there was a central, unnourished innocence in the way Watson pronounced the word East, and I saw that I would have to be careful or run the risk of destroying him entirely.

"Tell me exactly where you're going," I persisted.

"India, Japan," he waved vaguely.

"Alone?"

"Of course!"

"You're not taking anyone with you?"

"No one."

"Something's happened, Watson. Something you should know about."

"Is it really so important? I'm sure you can look after whatever it is."

"Seth is missing."

I watched his eyes; they blinked once, that was all. I remembered once years ago when Watson had seen a dwarf tapping his crutch by a bus stop; he had come close to weeping; something should be done, he had said. But the compulsion to relieve suffering was an abstraction for him, a folk belief in husk form. (Later I realized that outrage was only another form of innocence.) For a missing son he could only blink.

"I said Seth is missing."

"Missing?"

"Have you seen him, Brother Adam? Just tell me if you've seen him."

"No. Why would I see him?"

"Greta Savage has taken him. Taken him away."

"Greta Savage."

"We think . . . the police think . . . she's going to bring him here."

"Why would she do that?"

"Are you sure they didn't come here?"

"They wouldn't come here."

My throat closed with helplessness. Why did he have to speak in these dead, ritualized negatives? This convoluted room with its lights and mirrors and riotous grass was just another dead-end. I bent down for a moment and touched the tops of the grass. "You're leaving all this behind?" I asked.

"I'll take seed," he said, pointing to a suitcase beside the bed.

I stood up abruptly, and at that instant Watson's face

took on a startled expression. For the first time I became aware of a commotion down below on the street, a screeching of brakes, car doors slamming, people running on the road, some of them shouting. We heard too the sound of footsteps on the stairs of the house. Brother Adam rose with haste; the folds of his robe sighed around him.

Then, quite clearly, I heard Eugene's voice calling me. It seemed to come from the street. Or was it echoing up the stairwell? He was shouting something. It sounded like, "We've got Seth, Charleen, we've got him. We've got Seth and he's okay." I stood completely still. I had never, it seemed, listened before with this degree of intensity. There were more voices. And again there was the sound of running on the stairs.

Brother Adam picked up his suitcase, and with a sweep of his robe, he moved toward the fire escape. But he stopped there, staring at me for a moment as though waiting to be released.

"Charleen," was all he said. A question or a cry? Even afterwards I couldn't decide. Who was it who said that the sounds of our own names are the only recompense we have for the difficulties of living? I am certain, however, of one thing: that Watson didn't actually step out onto the fire escape until I nodded across at him. Then without a sound he dropped into darkness. I never even wished him good luck.

The next face I saw was Seth's. He burst into the room with Eugene behind him, absurdly off-hand in his tan windbreaker. My arms around him, his tumbled hair smelling of potato chips, his familiar face laughing at me above the brilliant jungle of living grass.

❧

Late Wednesday night. Some days are too long; it seems too much to ask of mere human beings that we

190

live through them. What we need, what *I* need, is release from today. I need sleep, darkness.

But I can't sleep. Consciousness is flaking away, but I'm still absorbing the various levels of unreality which have suddenly invaded my mother's Scarborough bungalow; I'm breathing them in, examining them, puzzling over their intricate folds and, like a classic insomniac, reliving all of it.

The policemen—they've all gone home now. How do policemen manage to get to sleep after a night like tonight? Of course, it's probably nothing to them; line of duty and all that; a ho-hum affair really; wouldn't even make the papers, one of them had told us.

Doug and Greta. It has been so simple in the end, so completely unspectacular. (Greta had simply driven up to the house and opened the car door. She never even suspected she was being followed.) How tender Doug had been with her. In the middle of the street with the searchlights and the beginning of a curious crowd, how gently he had held her, crooning into her hair, "It's okay now, baby, I'll take care of you, there now, don't cry like that." But she had cried. A small, animal weeping perforating the quiet neighbourhood, her thin shoulders shaking, "I don't know what I was doing. He was going to India. I wanted Seth to see him. I didn't know what to do. All I want to do is go to sleep."

"I know, I know," Doug had said. "You need to sleep. I'll take care of you now. You don't have to worry about anything."

Watson. No one had seen him come down the fire escape. No one knew where he went. "Too much confusion," one of the officers had said, rather embarrassed. "Anyway, it looks as though he wasn't involved."

"He was moving out anyway," the scrawny man told us. "Paid up his rent yesterday, but the bugger left all his

191

goddamn garbage behind. Lived there two years and you oughta see the goddamn junk he's got. A real nut, one of yer hopheads, oughta be in jail."

Watson living alone for two years! Watson, a crouching ascetic! How extraordinary really, considering his terrible need for an audience. (Then I remember the mirrors.)

Louis Berceau, another solitary—but his time is coming. What a lot he's giving up, the enormity of the sacrifice! Why? Why? His blissful detachment is ending; now he will be assaulted by all sorts of troubling concerns; his life will begin to overlap with others in ways which are not casual but responsible and which may throw into jeopardy his springy step and his childish good faith. Ah, Louis, sleep well tonight.

My mother who will be married the day after tomorrow: she has taken a sleeping pill. As soon as we came home with Seth, she announced that she was going to take a sleeping pill and go to bed. She explained that she does not normally indulge in such drugs. The doctor had given her these, but she takes them very sparingly. Only for pain and anxiety, she explained. Pain and anxiety: she pronounced these two words absently as though they amounted to nothing more than a case of indigestion, a stomach cramp, a twinge of heartburn. Judith and I exchanged wry looks. Only pain and anxiety? Was that all?

Judith and Martin. They are sleeping together in the back bedroom off the kitchen. Judith has been offhand but tactful. "Look, Char, it's not that I don't love you and all that, but as long as Mother's dead to the world—if you don't mind—the fact is, I just can't sleep soundly unless Martin and I are . . . you know . . . you get used to the feel of someone, and Eugene probably—"

Eugene, yes. Lying in my mother's veneer bed, his

arms around me—he is sound asleep now, but he has thought of everything: he has set his travel alarm for six-thirty so we can be sure to switch back before morning. He has also driven Greta to a hospital, found Doug a hotel room nearby, bought Bill Miller a bottle of rye. And checked Seth over for damages: "Of course I'm not a doctor, but there's nothing wrong with him that a good night's sleep won't fix."

And Seth is here in this house. Still a little baffled, a little confused—"I know it sounds crazy but she said you and Dad were getting back together again and she was supposed to take me to Toronto and I was too mixed up and half asleep. I guess I even believed her for the first day or two. It sounded like a dream, you know . . . like a wish come true."

"A wish? You mean you wished—?"

"Well, not exactly a wish—" He stopped, smiling suddenly, a self-mocking grin, but I could tell he was smiling at something else too, smiling at that swelling intangible that the "pome people" refer to as fate and others simply call life. It was a dazzling smile.

He was glad to see Eugene. Eugene is going to get him a plane ticket so we can fly back together Friday night after the wedding. The concert is Saturday; with luck they'll let him play even if he did miss a few rehearsals. He's in good spirits and went to sleep almost immediately.

And that's the most extraordinary thing of all: Seth is asleep in this house and he's sleeping where no one else has ever slept before, not my father, not Cousin Hugo, not Aunt Liddy, not Eugene, not anyone. Wound in a sheet and topped with a single blanket—for it is surprisingly warm tonight—he is sound asleep in the living room on my mother's sacred chesterfield.

The whole house, in fact, is asleep.

Chapter 7

Friday. My mother's wedding day. I wake up early and something whispers to me: get this right. Remember every detail. Be accurate, be objective, be thorough. Make a Chronicle of this, make a Wedding Album, get it Right. Begin with the cloud-crammed dawn, the sky oily-blue and unsettled. A heavy dew, a choking, webby haze. Around noon the sun nuzzles its way through, making the day exceptionally humid. A little cooler late in the afternoon. At six there is a brief downpour, at eight a swollen, streaky-eyed sunset, but by that time Eugene and Seth and I are on our way back to Vancouver and it's all over.

❦

We start the day by eating breakfast together, my mother and I, Eugene and Seth, Martin and Judith. Since there are only four kitchen chairs, Eugene carries in two from the dining room. It occurs to me that this is perhaps the largest number ever to gather in this room for breakfast.

We drink coffee—my mother allows for exactly two cups each—and eat buttered toast. "Margarine is cheaper," she reminds us, "but the day hasn't come when I can't afford a bit of butter in the morning."

There is a great deal of conversation around the table; the six of us are surprisingly comfortable together.

Eugene, laughing, tips his chair back slightly and fails to respond to my mother's sharp, disapproving glance.

My mother speaks to Seth—this grandson she scarcely knows, this grandson whose arrival has occasioned embarrassment and chaos but whose presence has somehow enlivened and restored the household—"I suppose you'd like some corn flakes for breakfast?"

"Yes," he answers, "if you have any."

"Well, I don't," she returns. "I refuse to spend good money on rubbish like that."

At this Seth laughs uproariously, as though his grandmother has said something exceptionally witty.

"What *you* need is a good haircut, that's what you need," she continues.

Seth claps his hands over his ears in mock horror. Or is it mock horror? I refuse to meet his eyes.

"Maybe you're right, Grandma," he says amiably, demonstrating his instinct for the inevitability of things. "I'll give it some thought."

"If I were you I'd give it more than thought," she retorts with spirit.

"I think there are some hedge clippers in the basement," Martin says.

We linger over our coffee with the languor of passengers on a steamship, the last leg of the journey in sight. The wedding looms ahead—three-thirty in my mother's living room—but even that event is overshadowed by the liberating awareness of our separate departures, the return to our other lives which, like real sea voyagers, we view with a mixture of reluctance and anticipation.

"Martin," Judith says after breakfast as she tidies my mother's kitchen, "did you see that thing in *The Globe and Mail* about the judge?"

"No," Martin answers, "what judge?"

"You know, that Supreme Court judge, old what's his-name. Seventy-six years old and getting married."

"Oh yes," Martin says, "I think I *did* see the headline."

"And he's marrying a woman about the same age. Second marriage for both of them."

"Hmmm," Martin comments.

"So it's not so odd really, people getting married in their seventies."

"Who ever said it was odd?"

"Maybe it's the coming thing."

"Maybe."

"It's logical, when you think of it," she says thoughtfully. "There's a nice—you know—economy to the whole thing. In fact, it sort of fits in with the recycling philosophy."

"Oh?"

"After all, here's Mother getting an escort and chauffeur. And Louis is getting a cook and housekeeper."

"Is that all?" Martin looks up amused.

Judith scours the sink with energy.

"Is that all?" Martin asks again. Then he starts to laugh.

"What's so funny?" Judith asks turning around.

But Martin is laughing too hard to answer.

My mother spent almost all morning at the hairdresser's.

It had been Judith's idea: "Look," she had reasoned with her, "you don't even have a hair dryer. And it's so damp this morning your hair will never dry. It would be a whole lot easier if you just went down to that little beauty place next to the Red and White. Eugene could drive you over, couldn't you Eugene? And you can have it washed and set and be back by noon."

"It's such a waste . . ."

"I'll phone right now and see if they can work you in. I'll explain . . ."

"There's so much to do here . . ."

"Charleen and I can tidy up the house. You have a nice restful morning under the dryer. I'll phone . . ."

"I don't know . . ."

"I'll ask if they can take you at ten-fifteen."

She had gone. Judith had won. It was in every way a sensible plan, but I had been appalled by my mother's quick surrender, her willingness to be led. This weakness is something new; she *is* getting old.

"She's getting old," I say later to Judith.

"Yes," Judith nods briskly. She is plugging in the old vacuum cleaner, and I watch as she attacks the living room rug. How realistic Judith is, how offhandedly she deals with the externals of life. She knows how to manage our mother, how to persuade her against her will, and she accepts her victories with stunning ease.

The vacuum cleaner is thirty years old, an upright Hoover with a monstrous black bag, and the sound of its roaring motor fills the house.

I picture my mother in the hands of a bullying shampoo girl in platform shoes, I think of the painful plastic rollers and the chemical sting, the scorching heat of the hairdryer, the futile aggression of *Harper's Bazaar,* and suddenly I am swept with a desire to rush out and find her and protect her. That is when it strikes me that I must . . . love . . . her in a way which Judith would never comprehend.

"It'll do her good to get out of the house," Judith yells over the roar of the vacuum cleaner.

❧

Yesterday morning Louis came to put in the shrubs I had bought. He worked slowly but with pleasure.

"Good healthy roots on this one," he said, patting the soil around a mock orange.

"I don't know why you thought I needed more bushes," my mother called to me crossly from the back door. "There are already more than I can look after."

"I like the smell of a mock orange," Louis said to me. "When it's in bloom it's the most wonderful perfume in the world."

After my mother went back into the house, Louis whispered to me, "Remember what we were talking about yesterday?"

"Yesterday?" I blinked.

"About that friend of yours. The priest."

I stared.

"You were going to ask him to come to the wedding."

"Oh," I breathed, "oh, yes, I remember."

"I've been thinking it over. And on second thought maybe it wouldn't be such a good idea after all."

"Oh?" I said.

"I appreciate it, I really do, but you know, a stranger and all," he paused and nodded almost imperceptibly toward the house, "maybe it wouldn't be such a good idea."

Later, when he had finished the planting, he went inside the house. He and my mother sat at the kitchen table talking a little and drinking coffee, Louis stirring in sugar, and my mother primly, awkwardly, perseveringly sipping. Seeing them sitting there like that I had a sudden glimpse of what their life together would be like. It would be exactly like this; there would be nothing mystical about it; it would be made up of scenes like this.

Not that I understand the complex equation they teeter upon, or the force that brought them together in the first place. It occurs to me that there are some happenings for which the proper response is not comprehension at all, but amazement and acceptance.

❧

Eugene drove my mother to the hairdresser's, and Seth, feeling restless, went along for the ride. While they are gone Judith and I vacuum and scrub, dust and polish. Martin, whistling, helps us wash the windows with vinegar and old newspapers. Then we stand back and regard the living room with its old, slipcovered chesterfield, its bulky armchairs, dark tables, heavy curtains and the rounded archway into the even gloomier dining room. It is scrupulously clean, but for all the crowding of furniture it looks barren, pinched and depressing.

"We'll put the lace table cloth on," Judith decides. "That should help a little."

Martin takes the tablecloth down from the top of my mother's linen cupboard, and throwing it over his arm, begins to tap out a soft cha-cha-cha. "Ta ta tatata, ta ta tatata," he sings as he whirls and swoops in the narrow space between the china cupboard and the dining room table. The tablecloth swirls and circles, cascading to the floor as he steps deftly and lightly around the chairs. "Down, down, down South America way," he hums to the lacy folds.

Judith smiles at him lazily. "You'll tear it, Martin, and then you'll catch it."

"Then I'll catch, catch, catch, catch it," Martin sings, dipping gracefully past us.

Judith takes the cloth from him and opens it on the table. "Well," she eyes the yellowed edges, "you can't say it looks exactly festive."

But then Eugene comes in the front door carrying armloads of spring flowers.

"Flowers!" I exclaim.

"I never thought of flowers," Judith marvels.

"Voila!" Martin cries, and, slowing to a cool elbow-spinning, shoulder-dipping softshoe, he shuffles into the kitchen to look for vases. For an instant—it couldn't have been more than a second really—I wish, feverishly wish, that I could dance away after him. I wish Judith would stop frowning and tugging at the edge of the tablecloth, and most of all I wish Eugene would stop standing there in the doorway, heavy and perplexed, with the tulips slipping sideways out of his arms.

Then Judith cries, "You're a genius, Eugene, I love you."

Then something happens: I look at Eugene in a frenzy of tenderness and begin to be happy.

❦

Yesterday afternoon Louis offered to cut the grass.

"It's too much work," my mother told him, "especially after putting in all those useless bushes."

"I'll cut the grass," Seth volunteered.

My mother considered, "Might as well keep busy," she said. "Idle hands . . ."

Seth laughed; he seems to find his grandmother's sayings shrewd and amusing. He carried the old hand mower up from the basement, oiled it carefully and began cutting back and forth across the tiny back lawn.

Watching him, I suddenly remembered the box of grass I had left behind in Vancouver, Brother Adam's grass. I had left it on the window sill, abandoned it without a thought, when I might easily have arranged for a neighbour to come in and water it. By the time I get home it will probably have turned brown; in all this heat it might even have died. How, I demanded of myself, had I been so neglectful?

The idea came to me that there may have been something willful in my oversight, that I may unconsciously have conceived a deathwish for my lovely grass, hating it while I pretended to love it. (The mind is given to such meaningless mirror tricks.) Had I subconsciously recognized Watson in those lengthy, grassy letters, had something about them touched a vein of familiarity, a flag of memory. Toying with these thoughts, I couldn't decide, but my aptitude for self-deception pressed me closer and closer toward belief. Poor Brother Adam, his love of grass which I had believed was prompted by an Emersonian vision of oneness, was only one more easy commitment, an allegiance to a non-human form, a blind and speechless deity. And poor Watson, his life hacked to pieces by his endless self-regarding; every decade a ritual pore cleansing, a radical, life-diminishing letting of blood. (After he had disappeared down the fire escape, after the excitement of seeing Seth had died down, I had picked up the book he had been reading; it was titled *The Next Life*.)

❧

It is a good thing Eugene kept the rented car because it turns out to be quite useful. At noon he picks up my mother from the hairdresser's and brings her home. Seth arrives a few minutes later by foot; he has had his hair trimmed and, smiling sheepishly, he allows us to admire him.

We eat sandwiches standing up in the kitchen, and then Eugene drives Martin and Judith to Union Station to meet their children who arrive on the one o'clock train.

I hardly know Meredith and Richard, and Seth has never seen them. Richard is shy, somewhat sulky, and, after three hours on the train, wild with hunger. Meredith at eighteen is beautiful. Judith has told me that her daughter's beauty has made her own aging bearable. "It's an odd consolation, isn't it?" she said. "You'd think I'd be jealous, but I revel in it."

201

Meredith kisses her grandmother with surprising force. "Well, how does it feel to be a bride again?" she bursts out.

"I was just going to lie down for my rest," my mother says in a wavy-toned way she has.

"Right now?" Meredith's eyes open wide.

"Just for an hour. I always have a rest after lunch, you know that."

"Hold it for five minutes, Grandma. I've got a surprise for you."

"A surprise?"

"You wait here. I'll set it up in the kitchen."

Meredith, shopping bag in hand, races into the kitchen opens her blue umbrella on the kitchen table, balancing it carefully on two spokes. Underneath it she arranges a dozen small parcels wrapped in silver paper and tied with pale pink ribbon.

"Okay now, Grandma. You can come in."

"What in the world . . ."

"It's a shower, Grandma, a kitchen shower."

"But I've got everything I need . . ."

"I know, Grandma," Meredith dances around the table, "but you're a bride, you've got to feel like a bride."

There is a new set of measuring cups in copper-tinted aluminum.

"But I have some measuring cups . . ."

"But they're all dented and ancient. I noticed last time we were here."

There is a new ironing-board cover.

"Now you can throw that old rag away." Meredith chortles.

There is a little needle-like device to prick the bottoms of eggs with.

"So they won't break when you boil them," Meredith explains.

"But all you have to do is add some salt . . ."

There is a wooden spoon. A new spatula. A twisted spring for taking lumps out of gravy. Two tiny soufflé dishes in white china.

"For you and Mr. Berceau," Meredith tells her joyfully, "and you can put them right in the oven."

There is a miniature ladle for melted butter. A painted recipe box made in Finland. And a beautiful, new streamlined egg beater with a turquoise plastic handle and whirling, purring, silvery gears.

"Lovely," everyone agrees.

"Just what you needed."

"Merangues, cakes . . ."

"—a beauty—"

"But I have an egg beater . . ."

"Grandma, smile. This is your wedding day, you're a bride."

❧

While my mother rests we set up the presents on the buffet. There aren't many. Judith and Martin are giving bedspreads.

"Two bedspreads?" I ask.

"Well . . . yes. One seemed sort of, you know, suggestive. I mean, that's the way she might see it. Two sort of cancels out the whole thing. One for the guest room and one for her room, more like a general refurbishing. God, I hate all this delicacy, but you know how she is, and the fact is, we couldn't think of anything else."

Eugene has bought them a kitchen radio which we think was rather an inspiration, a trim little model in white plastic with excellent tone and a year's guarantee. And since my shrubs hadn't been very successful, I decided yesterday to buy something else, something small but personal: I decided to give them my complete works, my four books of poetry.

Curiously enough my mother has never read anything I've written. She has, in fact, never expressed the slightest desire to do so, and a species of shyness has prevented me from ever sending her a copy. Furthermore, though she is not an astute reader, it has always worried me that she might comprehend something of the darkness in my poetry. It might wound her; it might remind her of something she would rather forget.

But now seemed like a good time to make a presentation. Like Judith, I had begun to know that I might never be able to talk to her. Who knows? Perhaps this was a way.

I had to buy the books retail by going to a bookstore and paying the regular price instead of getting them directly from the publisher as I normally do in Vancouver. Eugene and I went downtown yesterday to a very large bookstore, and there, in the poetry section, I found all four of my books. (They have recently been re-issued as a rather attractive set.) My picture in rainbow hues smiled happily at me from the back covers.

It was an altogether surreal experience to be buying my own books; I felt as though I were participating in a piece of cinema vérité. I felt, in fact, extraordinarily foolish placing those books in the hands of the cashier at the front of the store.

She checked the titles and then she turned the books over to check the price. Now, I thought, now she's going to suffer a brief instant of confusion; then her mouth will fall open in astonished recognition.

But none of this happened. Instead she took my twenty dollar bill, slapped it down on the cash register, sighed sharply, and snapped at me, "I suppose this is the smallest you've got."

"Yes," I said weakly, faintly, "I'm afraid that's all I have."

🌷

Meredith and Judith and I make three bouquets, one

for the dining-room table, one for the mantle of the artificial fireplace and a tiny one to set on the telephone table by the front door.

"Shouldn't we save some for Grandma's bouquet?" Meredith asks. "Or is Mr. Berceau bringing that?"

Judith and I stare at each other; neither of us had thought of a bridal bouquet. "Damn it," Judith bursts out, "I should have ordered something."

"Maybe Louis *will* bring one," I say, not very convincingly.

"Hmmmm," Judith says, "I doubt it."

"I don't suppose she could carry some of these tulips?" Meredith asks.

"Not really," Judith says, "tulips aren't quite the thing for a bridal bouquet."

"Maybe if we phoned a florist right away . . ." I begin.

"Lilacs!" Meredith says. "They'd be perfect."

"I don't know," Judith says doubtfully.

"They'd make a perfect bouquet," Meredith assures us, "and there are tons of them in the backyard. And they're at their best right now."

"Well," I say, "why not?"

"The only thing is," Judith hesitates, "well, you know how Mother always was about lilacs. They're just weeds, she used to tell us. Remember that, Charleen?"

"No," I reply, "I don't remember her ever saying that."

"We were always wanting to take a bunch to school— you know—flowers-for-the-teacher sort of thing. And she'd never let us because she said they were just weeds."

"I don't remember that," I say again, and saying it I am conscious of a curious lightening of heart. It is somehow wonderful and important to know that at least part of the burden of memory has been spared me.

"But lilacs are beautiful," Meredith protests, "they're heavenly flowers; I can't think of more gorgeous flowers. I'll make a bouquet for Grandma, just leave it to me," she says.

❧

Eugene, who is not normally introspective about his profession, just as he is not particularly critical or adulatory about it, once told me that he occasionally has moments when he is visited by a sharp sense of unreality. It happens most frequently when he is delivering to his young patients lectures on the importance of brushing their teeth. For a moment or two he feels himself undergoing a dizzying separation: suddenly he is the farmboy from Estevan eavesdropping on a solemn, middle-aged professional in a white jacket who is piously pressing for dental hygiene as though it were a system of morality. He is invariably self-amused when this occurs and at the same time awed by the transcendental experience of seeming to overhear himself.

I had something of the same feeling myself yesterday talking to my mother about Greta Savage; I had replied to her questioning with a calm I hadn't known I possessed, and hearing myself I had felt very close to being the person I would like to be.

"What are you going to do about that woman?" she asked.

"What woman?"

"That crazy woman. That kidnapper."

Without really intending to, I heard myself defending Greta, explaining to my mother that Greta had taken Seth as an act of love. She loves Seth, and, in a neurotic, labyrinthian way, she loves me too.

My defense of Greta was all the more surprising because I defended her instinctively. Like the kind people of the world—like Eugene-the-orthodontist—I had

206

judged with instant charity; like the good folk in fairy tales I had performed magic, spinning gold from straw, transforming apples to golden guineas. Kindness, kindness—a skill which I have nourished and rehearsed and worried into being—had jumped out and taken me by surprise. Without thinking, without laborious reflection I had fallen into its easy litany.

Even more surprising, it had given me a temporary ascendancy; my mother had been silenced; perhaps kindness and bravery have a common root.

"Greta acted out of love," I told my mother again, and, overhearing myself, I knew it was true.

�--

"Here comes Louis Cradle," Martin calls from the front window.

"Louis who?" I ask.

"Louis Cradle. And he's all zooted up."

Judith, setting out teacups, explains, "Berceau is French for cradle."

"Oh," I say, for an instant stung by my ignorance—how spotty my education was—was I going to spend a lifetime meeting such voids?

Louis Cradle, Mr. and Mrs. Cradle. Mentally I thrust about for the symbolism, cradle of a new life, no, too pat, the sort of pearl the "pome people" dived after—the "pome people" could never leave a paradox unturned, seeing life as a film strip jerking along from insight to insight, a fresh truth revealed every three and a half minutes—better forget about symbolism; yes.

Louis coming into the house looks no more dressed up than he was when he took me for lunch; indeed he wears the same old navy blue suit which does, however, look as though it has been brushed and perhaps even pressed.

But he is wearing a hat, a soft cloth cap in a fine wool,

rather a strange choice for so warm a day. Yet, the effect seems not unsuitable. I've often noticed that men who cover their heads, sweetly and solemnly concealing the tops of their heads with turbans, hoods, fezzes and skull caps, seem to be putting on a spiritual covering which announces piety and humility and which, in the short-hand of costume, declares that life is perishable, vulnerable and worthy.

At half past two my mother has her bath; then she retires to her room again in order to get dressed. The house is ready. Martin and Eugene have even managed to pry open one of the living room windows, long ago painted shut, and a breeze drifts in. The cake has been delivered, and there is a box of tiny, paper-thin cookies too. Judith and I arrange them on a tray; we put out milk and sugar, and I even set out a circle of lemon slices on a glass plate.

The only thing missing is a scene which I half-imagine might take place, the scene where my mother takes Judith and me aside and asks us if we object to the fact that she is remarrying, if we have any sensitivities about our father being more or less supplanted. Some faint, quivering, awkwardly-delivered apology, a seeking of approval or even permission, at the very least a fumbling for consensus or a simple explanation: she is lonely, she needs someone to look after the furnace, see to the insurance, someone to talk to. But now it's almost time for the wedding. The missing scene is clearly not going to take place; thank God, thank God.

"Where's Grandma?" Meredith asks us.

"Getting dressed," I say nodding at the closed door.

The minister has arrived, a young man, no more than twenty-five, with a prominent bridge of bone above his eyes; his face gleams with sweat. "Hot day for May," he announces nervously.

"Wonderful, isn't it?" Judith says a little defiantly. She has changed to a striking sleeveless dress in rough, lemon-coloured cloth.

"Perhaps you'd be more comfortable if you took off your jacket," suggests Martin, who does not intend to wear a jacket.

"My mother will be out in a minute," Judith says. "She's just getting dressed."

"This really is a happy occasion," the young man remarks.

Louis, supremely relaxed and almost dapper, invites him to sit down by the window. "It was very good of you to agree to come."

"Do you think I should see if Grandma needs a hand?" Meredith whispers to me.

"No. She'll be out in a minute," I answer.

"It's half past three."

"Really?"

"On the dot."

"Not like her to be late."

"Especially for her own wedding."

" . . . really should check, don't you think?"

"Give her a minute or two."

"You're sure she's all right?"

"Maybe we should . . ."

"Ah, there she is now."

"Mother."

"Mrs. McNinn?"

"Oh, Grandma!"

"My dear."

❧

The ceremony, a shortened version of the traditional marriage service, is performed in front of the artificial fireplace (symbolism?) and, since it is short, we all remain standing. Judith and Martin stand in the archway to the dining room, Eugene and I by the window, and the three children beside the television set.

My mother's voice repeating the vows is exceptionally matter of fact. She might be reading a recipe for roast beef hash, and curiously enough, I find her lack of dramatic emphasis reassuring and even admirable. Louis, on the other hand, seems quite overcome. He chokes on the words and once or twice he dabs at his eyes, though this may be the result of asthma rather than emotion.

From where I stand I can see only their backs; my mother leans slightly to the left; perhaps her operation has unbalanced her. And Louis stoops forward as though anticipating an attack of coughing. They look rather fragile as people always do from the rear; it is after all the classic posture of retreat. Retreat from what? Age, illness, loneliness? Louis slips a ring on my mother's hand and they stand for a moment with hands joined. Two is a good number, I think, and like a chant it blocks out the remainder of the service for me. Two is better than ten; two is better than a hundred; two is better than six; when all is said, two is better than one; when all's said, two is a good number.

❧

"That's a lovely bouquet you're carrying, Mrs. McNinn. Oh, I'm so sorry, I should have said Mrs. Berceau."

"Well, lilacs aren't my favourite, but my granddaughter here . . ."

"Won't you have some tea, Louis?"
"Yes, please, Judith, that's just what I need."
"And a piece of cake?"
"A nice cake, isn't it?"
"You weren't a bit nervous, were you, Louis?"
"Well, to tell you the truth—"

"Welcome to the fold, Louis."

"Well, well, thank you, Martin, very kind of you."

"Great institution, marriage."

"Do you think she's holding up okay, Char?"

"She looks a little tired. But not bad."

"Considering . . ."

"Nice you could come east with Aunt Charleen, Eugene."

"I wouldn't have missed it, Meredith."

"You're just being polite."

"No, really."

"What do you think, Judith, should I bring out the champagne?"

"I don't know, Martin. You know Mother. What do you think?"

"I don't know. Oh, hell, why not?"

"And that woman over there? Mrs. Forrest? She's your aunt, is that right?"

"Yes, she's a poet. Most people think we look alike."

"And the man with her? Dr. Redding? In the grey suit?"

"That's Eugene. Her lover."

"Lover?"

"You look so shocked. Are you really shocked?"

"Of course I'm not shocked. Why should I be shocked?"

"You must have been scared getting kidnapped like that."

"Scared?"

"I mean, did you think she was going to try for ransom or something like that?"

"Naw, it wasn't like that. It was—I don't know—it was kind of fun, the whole thing."

"You look beautiful, carrying that bouquet."

"Have some more cake, someone has to eat all this cake."

"It's good cake."

"A little dry, if you ask me."

"May I propose a toast . . ."

"Good idea."

"I've never had champagne before."

"Neither have I."

"Really?"

"Delicious."

"Like ginger ale, only sour."

"Ah, look at the bubbles rising."

"You're supposed to *sip* it, Richard."

"Here, have another glass, Judith."

"If you're sure there's enough . . ."

"Lovely."

"Tea is plenty good enough for me."

"Here's to marriage."

"Here's to the bride and groom."

"Here's to the future."

"Happy days."

❧

"I love you, Eugene."

"Charleen, Charleen."

Nothing is what it seems. Our plane flying west is defying a basic natural law which says that on any given day the sun sets only once; but here it is setting over

Lake Superior, again over Winnipeg, over the prairies, over the mountains. We're diving into its fiery, streaming trail, we're chasing it down to its final, almost comic, drowning. *Don't tell me about the curve of the earth.*

Eugene, peering down through grey mist, says, "What we should do is buy a farm. A few acres. For weekends, you know. Maybe grow some vegetables, have a horse for the kids. Might even be a tax advantage there . . ."

My childhood is over, but at the same time—and this seems even more true—it will never be over. Say it fast enough and it sounds like a scuttling metaphysic of survival. *Who ever said you can't live without logic.*

"Ladies and gentlemen," a voice says, "this is your captain speaking." *But how do we know it is our captain?*

"We've just been told there's a light rain over Vancouver—" *A light rain, a light rain, the beginning of a poem, a light rain.*

"But visibility is excellent—" *Watch out for symbolism now.*

"We hope you have enjoyed your flight. This is your captain wishing you a good evening." *Good evening, good evening.*